Hidden Death

A Matt Smith Mystery

David E. Tienter

HIDDEN DEATH
By
DAVID E. TIENTER
Copyright ©
David E. Tienter 2016

Edited by Jennifer Zipperer
Cover Illustration by DatDesigns a fiverr certified seller

Printed in the U.S.A.

ISBN-13: 9781530284535
ISBN-10: 1530284538

Dedication

A special thanks to Connie and Steve Haar, and to Daniel Wyatt for providing the legal help. I also want to thank my wife, Anne. Without her continuing help and encouragement I could not have completed this work.

Table of Contents

1
The Gambler

AT TIMES, THE big empty closes in too hard on me. The pressure pushes in as self is squeezed out, tiny pieces of ethereal Matt drift off into the mist. Through the years I've learned what helps me battle back against it, and now I'm surrounded by shelves of books with their cumulative wisdom and electronic distracters with their moronic life sucking issue. Still, tonight my overriding thought is: I've got nothing down on anything. I'm dying in here with too much life out there. Action. I need action on something. I'm forced to move from soft overstuffed to hard bar stool.

It's the overpowering pain of my reality crashing hard against a stone wall, built by the knowledge of man over the last 5000 years. I feel I have read every book, weighed every argument, but the lines all stretch to the same tedious ending, an argument which I cannot solve, and I cannot snap those lines or even stretch them a tad without destroying some of my tenuous grip on life. No matter the cost, my empty needs a bet down now. It has become overpowering.

Fuck it, fuck it, I got to go. Three long months I've held it in control, and for three months it's been building power. Enough, I absolutely know I can dodge one more bullet. I slip on my shoes, throw on a jacket, and I'm off to my local bar.

The Blue Bayou is the place I usually go. Great name for a dark, dumpy bar with no jukebox, that smells of rancid sweat and stale beer. Main thing that keeps it open is the in-house bookie. Commuters contribute to its upkeep between five and seven by stopping in for a quick two dollar pop of whiskey with a short glass of beer, to keep them fired for the ride home. After that, it's drunks, panhandlers who got ahead a couple of bucks, gamblers, and assorted strange losers who make up the lower layer of society in downtown Chicago. It has a stained wooden, beat-up bar, about ten yards long. A yellowing, cracked mirror covers the wall behind the bar. There are three cheesy little tables, each with four wooden chairs and fifteen stools, covered with cracked green plastic, pushed against the bar.

On the stool next to me tonight sits Ottis, a man who has solved his problems, slipped his burden, and found a way to say that which has to be said, without the disapproval of the world. He screams, grimaces, mouths, and whispers the deepest secrets of his being to his drink. The first couple of times I saw him, he freaked me out; now he's kind of a fixture.

He seems startled when I ask, "How's things tonight, Ottis?" He jerks back, eyes wide. Looks at me without comprehension, then regains his composure, turns, and again pours forth his silent lament to his as yet untouched drink. I've watched Ottis over the last five years and have never heard a sound issue from his lips to another person nor have I ever seen him finish a drink.

When Larry comes over, I order three shots of gin, three bottles of beer, and tell Larry to put a K on the Knicks tonight. Larry turns to look at the very large black man sitting at the right end of the bar.

"You been gone some time now, Matt. You sure you want to start the merry-go-round again?"

"Damn, T-Bo, you turning social worker? You know I always pay."

"Take it," nods T-Bo to Larry. "Some people learn hard. Just be in to pay up tomorrow, by two."

"Pay up by two, pay up by two. You ever think about learning a new song?"

"Don't be jacking your jaws at me, Matt. Best remember this is business, we not friends."

Gambler's rule number one: don't piss off your bookie. I turn back to my drinks, line them up neatly in a soldierly formation. I used to order scotch shots but scotch seems too ruggedly masculine of a drink, and it leaves no hangover in the morning. With no suffering later, this would indeed be a totally futile voyage into self-destruction. After all, we must pay for our sins.

Tonight is one of the unusual nights. There are two younger couples crowded together around the far end of the bar. Noisy and self-important as only twenty to thirty year olds can be, they shout down the bar at me several times, but I ignore them. Anyone who would bring a woman into this place is too stupid for me. I realize I may be wrong, they may be sociologists here to do research on the pond scum that frequents shitholes.

First I start with the small glasses. "Gin, the sorrow of a thousand English Mothers." It slides down smooth. I choke, gasp, take a drink of beer, then quickly down the other two gins. Take another long pull off the beer, finish it, and swallow the second cold frosty in two long gulps. Down to my last beer, I take out a cigar: a cigarillo, of course. Otherwise I wouldn't look like Clint. I lean back on my stool and light a match. The end begins to glow. I draw my first mouthful and pick up my beer.

"Goddammit, Matt, you know there is no smoking in here. How fucking many times you gotta get fined?" He's huffing up the bar at me. Larry's a good bartender. Well, as good a bartender as you could reasonably expect in a place that only serves shots and beer. He probably would be a friend if I treated him better. I really have no need for and don't want any friends.

"Listen to me, asshole," I tell him as I throw two twenties on the bar, "Go call your poor dying mother and it'll be out when you get back." He grumbles as he picks up the forty and wanders down to the end of the bar.

The beer is gone, the gin is buzzing, the cigarillo smoked down half-way. The anxiety of listening to my muffled drum with its numbered quotient of beats begins to recede. The years and cares begin to fall from my shoulders and for a short time life begins to again be appealing. Perhaps there can still be magic."Put out the damn cigar. Cause I have no trouble beating the crap out of an old shithead."

I turn and the two guys who had been sitting down the bar with the skirts are right behind my stool, probably trying to impress the ladies. I understand totally, cute blonde dollies are one thing that needs to be impressed. If I put out the cigar and quietly leave the bar, I will probably be okay. The bet is down, and I'm a little sloshed. However, one of the bad things about being a gambler is that I take stupid chances. I turn to look at studly dude number one. He appears to be a useless lifeform who has dedicated his life to irritating people. I decide I can take a little pain.

First I look away, then tilt my head down slightly to look at the floor. I sigh, like I'm a sorry little worm, swivel, drive my fist past the big talker, and land it flat onto the nose of studly guy number two. It's a good shot. Lands flush about halfway through the punch. My arm drives it another six inches before it completes its forward motion. My weight is 220 pounds and the swivel was fast, the punch righteous. That much force is usually more than a drunk, or in this case a useless piece of cow flop, can handle. He sails backward with blood spurting and crashes into a table. He ends up on the floor of the bar after some more crashing and thrashing around.

Studly one's first mistake was in thinking he could impress the dollies by bullying an old man who would not fight back. His second mistake is turning to watch his buddy go down. Curiosity is a killer in a fight. He doesn't see me pick up the beer bottle, and when he looks back at me, it smashes into his teeth. His hands fly to his face, and I kick him swiftly in the crotch. He moans softly and bends slowly to the floor holding his mouth with one hand and covering his genitals with the other. I'm sure he will feel better in a couple of days.

My right hand hurts from the punch and I shake it several times, before I stick the cigar back in my mouth and walk slowly toward the door. Hearing a loud thump, I look back to see that one of the peroxide blondes has crashed to the floor behind me. Apparently Ottis saw her running at me with a beer bottle in her hand and tripped her.

I hear the only words I will ever hear Ottis say, "Noisy bitch."

The next morning, I am motionless, sprawled on my bed. Damn phone rings. My head hurts and the damn phone is ringing. Sun burnt sow bellied son of a bitch, who in the fucking seven shades of crotch rot hell is calling me this early? I flop around until I can reach the wailing instrument of torture.

"Whatcha need?" I groan.

"Matt, it's Larry down at the Blue Bayou. How you doing?"

"Not worth a shit. Give me a few hours, and if I live I'll call you back." I hang up. Crawl out of the sack, grab a cup out of the sink, one that doesn't look too dirty, fill it with water, and drink deeply. "Dehydrated man arising." I drink another cup of water. Chest hurts when I breathe, shoulders just hurt. My right hand feels like I broke a few bones. Cough up a bunch of yellow crap and spit it down the drain, pour a half cup of bourbon, suck it down quick, and then drink another cup of water. Light a cigar, inhale deeply, and begin to feel better.

"Holy shit and hooray, I'll live to see another day." I open the door to let Bogie out. He handles his business quickly and races back for breakfast. He's a little mixed mutt who showed up hungry at my door a couple of years back. He's small and clean, fits into my three room apartment nicely.

"Hey little buddy, let's go out for chow. Whatcha think?" I head for the car and he's right behind me. He doesn't understand a lot, but he comprehends chow. I go through the carry-out window, then drag the food to an outdoor table. The little guy loves pancakes and eggs. They are gone in a minute. I have a biscuit with egg and sausage. Then start on the coffee. It's another absolutely beautiful day in Paradise, made for older people with a growing list of pains and a shrinking list of days. I have assessed all bodily functions and find that entity Matt has again started to enjoy life. Later at home the telly, via Robin Meade, tells me the Knicks have won. All good.

Off to the Blue Bayou at two. The sun's in the sky, and I'm riding high. One neat thou waiting for me. I'm looking forward to seeing T-Bo. The minor god of chance is being held prisoner in my back pocket. There's nothing now I can't win. I have to a new bet down on something. Larry sets me up a draught and T-man slowly counts out ten crisp bills.

"Way to pick 'em, Matt."

"What's going tonight?　Something I can double this chicken scratch up on."

"Got nothing till Tuesday 'cept the horses."

"Fuck, fuck, fuck," I say. "I'm hot now and I hate the ponies."

"Well," says T-Bo, "I'm hired muscle at a dog fight this afternoon. That put fire in your blood?"

"A dog fight? Never been.　Can they take my action?"

"Easily.　Plus, as long as I am there, you are safe.　No one ever fucks with T-Bo."

"Hell yeah, count me in.　You driving?"

"T-Bo don't give rides to dicks; bitches only in T-Bo's Jag." His Jaguar is emerald green.　He keeps it parked right outside the Blue Bayou where he can keep an eye on it. Every week or two some young lady hangs her panties over his antenna. He checks them out, and if they are looking good enough he offers to take them for a ride. T-Bo is not into romance but he likes biology.

"Watch my beer, Larry, be right back."

I've never been to a dog fight, but if I want to get a bet down today, I need to get my own wheels and go with T-Bo.　Within ten minutes I am back at the Bayou sucking at my suds again. When T-Bo motions to me, I go. I have a fifteen year old Explorer. Reliable but I never find panties hung around my antenna, and that's alright with me. By the time I was twenty, I had figured out that cute don't mean crap. Only people matter. Any woman who would be interested in having sex with me because of a grand auto, doesn't matter to me.

It takes a good twenty minutes down the Dan Ryan and then into the back streets. I'm placing us somewhere near Blue Island. He pulls up to a near-death garage with paint peeling off it. I slide in next to him. Follow him into the garage.

It's pandemonium with about forty Mexicans and black men already crushed but still milling around in the small garage. They all turn to look at the one white beamish face in the crowd.

T-Bo makes it clear. "He with me."

They all stop looking at me. The stale air has the acrid smell of fear, excitement, and fresh blood. The crowd parts as if by magic for T-Bo. I stay in his wake. He stops next to the money man. "Put your cash with Digger here. He be head man."

I give him the thou, betting on number two, a shit brindle brown pit weighing 70-80 pounds. Odds are two to one on the brown, I figure the big dog has a decided advantage in weight and muscle. The other dog is white with a pink nose looking to weigh in at 50 pounds. So far, I am quite interested in everything. The pit man is a short thin guy, looks to be Thai or Vietnamese. He raises his hand, and looks at the handlers. "Ready?" he asks, then brings his hand down, and the corner men let the dogs go.

I've seen horrific things in my life. Nothing else even comes close to the ferocity of these two animals. They each leap at the other's faces with bared fangs. Completely silent they tear at each other. The brindle struggles for a few seconds to get a good foothold, then easily pushes the white over onto his back. The little dog already has one ear almost torn off. Incredibly he stays game and rips at the brindle's stomach with his legs, trying to dislodge the bigger dog, who snaps at one of the back legs and crushes the bones. The sound is horribly deafening. Within seconds, the brindle has the smaller dog on his back and is tearing at his throat. His owner, a young man screams, "Stop it." The pit man nods, and the two owners enter the pit and pull their dogs apart by their rear legs. The money winners roar in approval. The losers shout to let the fight go on. A pit bull fight should go to death.

Money is changing hands, and several scraps break out in the crowd. T-Bo stops all the fights with a word.

Hooray, I've won. With my new fist full of money, I also collect a new feeling of shame and disgust. I feel an intense dislike for all of mankind. Only soulless beasts could arrange a fight between innocents. I collect my money and leave the garage. The cooler outside air helps, and I no longer feel the overpowering need to vomit. This hadn't been sport. This was the most vicious display of man and his greed, I have ever witnessed.

As I walk to my car, I see the young man leaning over and petting his dog. The kid isn't much but knobby knees, elbows, and uncut hair. With a face streaked by tears, he keeps saying, "You a good boy. You did good, Thunder." Thunder watches him, wagging his tail.

I want to beat the kid, break his leg, tear his ear off. I start toward him but realize immediately that the injuries to his dog are hurting him more than I could.

I ask the kid if he wants help getting the dog to a vet.

"He got a broken leg, mister, and he lost. Dog loses a fight, you gotta put him down."

"No. You can't put him down. That dog charged into hell for you, and now you want to kill him. Christ, only a fool would blame that dog for losing. You're the one at fault, you mismatched him. You don't want him, I will give you five hundred for him, because I'm taking him to a vet, now. You can come along or you can take the money and stay here, but that is too good a dog to be put down for a broken leg. Want to come or you want the five?"

"Just fuck off, mister. I got nothing but that dog and the clothes I'm wearing. How am I paying a vet?"

"Not your worry. I pay for my mistakes. Now get him in the car."

He picks up the bloody piece of white fur gently, trying not to hurt him, and carries him to my Explorer. I have my doubts that he will live, but feel we have to try to save him. He has such a big heart. The kid sits in the backseat with the dog in his lap, murmuring words of love and encouragement to the injured dog and rubbing his back.

"What's your name son?"

"D'Angelo."

"I'm Matt. When we get there, let me do the talking. Just be there if I need you, but don't say nothing."

I remember that the emergency vet at 128th and Western is open on Sunday. I had to have Bogie treated there one weekend. D'Angelo carries Thunder, while I ring the bell and knock on the door, trying to get their attention.

The tech finally opens to the door and lets us in.

"My dog got hit by a car," I say to the tech. "I think his back leg is broken."

The tech takes one look. "Oh yeah, never heard that before, got hit by a car. Was he fighting another dog when the car hit him?"

I reach into my pocket. Give him one bill. "Look more like a car accident to you now?" I ask.

No reply but he begins doing the paperwork. "Minimum charge for a traumatic injury is $290."

"Okay, just treat him good, he's my baby." I give him three more bills. He looks at me like I'm covered with maggots and not deserving to live, but he picks up Thunder gently and carries him into the back. I can accept him believing I'm scum, especially after today, as long as he treats Thunder good.

Thirty long minutes before a lady vet calls us to the back. A doped up Thunder tries to wag his tail, he can just move it a little. Vet shows us an x-ray. Leg has two breaks, lucky it missed his knee joint or we would probably be taking off that leg. We can set and cast it, clean up everything else, and sew his ear back on. It'll run right at $700."

"In addition to the $290?" I ask.

"Yes, the $290 was for initial exam, blood chemistries, and sedation."

"Well let's get him fixed up then."

The benches are hard cold plastic. D'Angelo sits across from me. The tables are stacked high with pictures of previous patients. The air is thin. It's hard to breath.

"Looks like he'll live. You gotta take care of him though, or he'll end up with an infection and die. You got a place to keep him clean and dry tonight?"

"Yeah, I'm staying under the railroad bridge down on 116th. I'll put him on my blanket."

I'm silent for a couple of minutes thinking, weighing options. "Nope, that's unacceptable. He won't make it two days under a rail-road bridge. Other dogs know he's injured, they'll kill him. Let me take him to my place until his cast comes off, then I'll bring him back to you."

We sit and look at each other for a good half hour. They bring out Thunder. He looks funny with his ear sewn back on and a bright orange cast on his leg. The tech places him gently into D'Angelo's arms while I pay. We get a bottle of pain pills, antibiotics, and a list of post-op instructions.

I'm unsure about my next move, could be making a big mistake, but a gambler goes in for a dime, he might as well go in for a dollar. "Listen D'Angelo, I'm making my invitation for you also. You can stay with me tonight, and take care of your dog. Got a couch for you and a blanket for him. You'll both be warm and dry. He's going to have to eat in the morning."

"I don't think so, buddy. For all I know, you one of them weird fuckers likes to bring young men home."

"I like girls, D'Angelo. And for the thousand I just spent getting your dog patched up, I could have twenty good looking ones in my bedroom tonight. But here's the thing, my saying it don't make it, so you got to take a chance just like I'm taking a chance on you. You might be one of those hopped up killers who's trying to get older white men alone to rob them."

We both sit quietly and look at each other. Trust is hard.

"I ain't no hop head and you don't look rich enough for me to rob."

"I'm pulling over to that stand and getting some tacos. You want some?"

I get a dozen tacos. Set them between us and start eating. "Help yourself if you want any. I need two for me and two for my dog."

He's pretty strong, he waited three blocks before he ate the first taco. When I pulled over by the bridge, I told him again he was welcome to come with me to make sure Thunder got good treatment.

"I've decided I will. For Thunder's sake, I will."

"Do you need to stop to get anything?"

"No, I got nothing here but half of a worn-out blanket and a can of beans. Someone probably stole the beans."

"There's still four tacos waiting to be eaten."

"Sure hate to let 'em go to waste."

At my place, I say, "Wait here a minute, be right back." I put Bogie on a leash, grab a towel for Thunder, and go back down.

"Okay now, wrap the towel around his tummy and lift the ends to support his back legs. That way he can do his business here. I give the last two tacos to Bogie, he walks next to Thunder with no trouble. They seem to accept each other right off

"Towel is a good idea, Matt."

"I've had a lot of dogs, learn stuff as you get older."

Back in my three room flat, I put down a blanket for Thunder, and give a pillow and blanket to D'Angelo. "Hope that couch is okay. See you in the morning."

I lock my bedroom door that night. In the morning, I throw on a pot of coffee, couple of pork chops, scramble a dozen eggs, and make a plate of toast. D'Angelo is sleeping on the floor. Thunder has the couch and pillow. I nudge D'Angelo's foot. "Better take the patient out for a walk. Hurry, food is on."

I eat a chop, a spoonful of eggs, and the rest is split into thirds amongst the dogs and boy.

"What are your plans now?" I ask.

"I am hoping you'll give me a ride back to the bridge."

"What the hell, you getting tired of my company already?"

"You know that isn't it, Matt. It's just you done so much for us already. Don't want to be beholden to you."

"I get tired of you, I'll give you the boot, don't worry. In the mean-time, this is what I suggest. We get some of those dividers, the kind you can move around, and make you a room there in the corner. We need one of those beds you can sit on too. I think they call them futons. Some groceries, and real food for Thunder, and a leash and a collar. Some underwear for you, and a couple of sets of decent clothes. You starting to smell. Right now my funds are limited, but if we go to Goodwill, and shop carefully, we might get it all. That puppy is going to need a nurse for the next couple of weeks, and I'm figuring you're the best nurse he can have. Only thing I ask is that you lock the door when you go out, and stay out of my bedroom."

D'Angelo takes a sip of coffee. "You one great cook, Matt. I like your plan lots better than mine." He reaches over to pat Thunder who is sitting next to him. That is one beautiful dog.

We head into the living room, click on the telly, and begin watch-ing a western. Halfway through the movie, I notice the big empty has completely left my chest. I look down. Thunder is resting his head on my leg and looking up at me with as much love as I have ever felt.

2
The Killer

IT WAS THE standard, brilliant blue sky with puffy white clouds day, in small town America. A sunny Sunday, early in the afternoon. The local people who were able had gathered in mass at Memorial park for fellowship and good will. No one wanted to miss the joyous celebration.

The killer was moving in the small town. The only thing he could hear was the "wheewha' wail of the old microphone the mayor was using to give his speech. He walked slowly along the deserted maple tree-lined streets of Tindale. He was dressed in worn faded denim shorts and a raucously flowered Hawaiian shirt; leisure clothes he used to camouflage the thirty extra pounds he carried around his tummy. Standing a little over six feet tall, he did not look grossly overweight. His head was bare, and he frequently raised his hand to provide shade for his eyes. When he had seen that Slug was being arrested, he had slipped his cap off and shoved it into a garbage bin. He knew he might need an excuse to get away.

He cracked the top off a cold beer, leaned over to his wife, and murmured that he needed to return home to get his cap. He walked toward the cement block rest rooms, slipped behind them and as inauspiciously as possible, made straight for the jail.

The activities at the park were in full swing with the tables, moved from city hall, loaded with potato salad, brats, and ambrosia salad, still sitting out. He had started eating right at noon with most of the other people. He walked around, talking with those he knew, politicking as his wife called it. The coolers full of ice, were overfull with beer and soft drinks. Horse shoes were flying down near the river's edge, flung by old men in coveralls and chambray shirts with rolled up sleeves. A work-up game of softball had started. With luck, none of these local yokels would miss him for the short time he would be gone.

The killer knew this was business which had to be settled now. He was a thinker, a planner who disliked having his hand forced, but Slug's arrest was doing just that.

With the celebration fully underway, the streets of the small town looked empty. Hopefully no one would notice him walking alone. The opportunity had presented itself, and he was forcing himself to pursue it now. Fighting nerves and cursing his bad luck, he concentrated on keeping his walk slow. Skittish, he checked his watch. Only four minutes had gone by, still plenty of time not to be missed.

From the corner of Elm and Main, where he stood in the shadow of a large maple tree, he could easily see the back of Sheriff Thatcher's head through the front window of the small jail. He figured that Thatcher was looking down at his portable television set watching the Vikings play. He disliked that he would have to kill Thatcher, but saw no way around it.

Sheriff Thatcher had let the rest of his crew attend the picnic with their families. The prisoner, James, was his stepson, and Thatcher felt it was his duty to take the watch. His small town responsibility complex wouldn't let his misfortune ruin the celebration for his deputies. They would spend the day with their families, enjoying the picnic and spreading good will for the department.

The tall man leaned casually against the tree and lit a smoke. Main street was being repaired. No workers were here on Sunday.

Piles of gravel and stone lay ready for them. Fresh tar was spread across the north side of the street, and he took a minute to figure out how to get through this obstacle. He had been gone for five minutes now. Perhaps he should return to the picnic before he was missed or his wife became suspicious. He palmed his .32 caliber preparing to shoot Thatcher as soon as he entered the office. He started walking toward the building, working his way around the obstacles. Then a stroke of luck, he saw the sheriff start to lean forward preparing to stand. The killer continued across the street purposely-not too fast, not too slow-just in case there was someone watching.

"Great timing," he thought, entering the office of the jail just as Thatcher closed the toilet door. Inside the office he quickly snatched the keys from the top drawer of the old gray desk, reclosed the drawer, walked through the locked door to the cell-block, and saw Slug lying on a cot.

The prisoner's head was propped up with a bare gray-white pillow. His eyes watched the tall man suspiciously. "What the fuck's up with you showing up here?"

"John said I could come in and talk for a minute. I just wanted to explain my side of it so you could understand maybe," he replied, unlocking the cell door. "Here, you want a smoke?" He threw a pack of Camels to Slug who caught them, extracted one neatly, and stuck it between his lips. "There isn't never going to be no understanding cause nothing you say can change shit, but thanks for the cig. Gotta light?" He looked up to the taller man.

Searching in his pocket for a lighter, the killer pulled out his old Zippo. He was proud of it and the condition he kept it in. He flipped the top open, blew gently on the wick, and spun the flint wheel. The flame burst forth and he stepped toward Slug holding the lighter. Slug stepped closer with his cigarette to get a light and pushed its tip into the flame.

Still groggy from sleep and alcohol, the man had difficulty holding his hand still enough to get a light easily. As he concentrated on the flame, the bigger man stepped behind him, encircled the short man's neck with his arm, twisted Sluggo's head slightly to the left, and pulled his right arm, still holding the lighter against the smaller man's throat. Pushing downward with his left hand, he snapped Slug's neck with one fluid motion. He carried the dead man, still jerking in his death spasm, to the cot, laid him on it, picked up the dropped cigarette, and heard the toilet flush. He knew he had to hurry now, and ran to the rear door with the keys, unlocked it, propped it slightly open with his lighter, then rushed back to the cell, wiping his prints off the keys with the tail of his Hawaiian shirt. He tossed them next to the dead prisoner, closed the door to the cell with his forearm and hurried back out the rear door. Inside of five minutes, he was back at the Memorial Park picnic.

"I thought you were going back to the house to get a hat," said his wife, looking at his still uncovered head.

"Yeah, I know, but I took a massive dump and forgot the damn hat on the way back. I started cramping up about a block from the house and had to hustle to make it. Apparently, I can't think of two things at once anymore. Hey," he said, taking her hand, "want to walk down by the river with me you gorgeous hunk of woman?"

3
The Gambler

RIGHT AFTER MY wife passed, on the advice of my Pastor, I joined a bereavement support group. We met in the basement of the Sacred Heart Catholic Church. The first night I just sat and watched, but at the second meeting I attended, I told the group how after forty years, it was hard to cook only one breakfast or pour only one cup of coffee. I did get a lot of support although I think it might have been because of the ten of us at the meeting, eight were widowers. Still I felt better when the meeting was over.

During the next week, prior to the meeting, I rethought everything that was said and how I felt. The truth of the matter came to me before the next session. I am not a sharing person. I certainly don't like talking about my feelings with strangers, and I don't want to go to a meeting, nor become attached to another woman. I don't need either a nurse or a purse, and I'm happy with just my own company. The wonderful woman I still love is enough for me, even though she's passed. The afternoon of the next meeting, I noticed in the newspaper that Dave Brubeck was in town. Instead of the meeting, I went to his concert. One night of truly magical jazz did more to raise my spirits than pouring my sorrow out to a group of strangers who would never understand the loss I had sustained. I know for me personally, pouring a cup of coffee for D'Angelo is more satisfying. He's company even if he doesn't talk much.

For the first three days he was here, I made the meals: meatloaf, pork chops, and a stewed beef. He always ate whatever I put down without a complaint. The fourth night I ordered pizza from Beggar's, a local joint with a high quality product. I took a slice, salted it a little, put on some red pepper flakes, and finally ate one bite. D'Angelo had already gone through three pieces. He went after that pizza like a mongoose after a cobra. He had scraped the debris off the plate by the time I consumed my one piece.

After that, we settled into a routine of pizza three days a week, burgers and dogs twice a week, and the other two nights, I cooked. I still made a salad every night, and the fruit was still vanishing, so there had to be some good nutrition going into us. I've been told by reputable sources that the soil is depleted. With the food train taking time to get to us, we don't get much nutrition from our food, but I'll be damned if I am going to buy supplements to keep me healthy. Anyway, I figure there's a lot of good stuff from the hops in the beer I drink.

D'Angelo spent most days on the computer. I suspect he is playing Pac Man or some other computer game, and it wouldn't surprise me much if there is now a porno site on my computer. I had been surprised when he asked if he could use it.

"You know how?"

"Sure, library has them. Used to spend a lot of time there keeping warm and dry. That was before I got Thunder, of course."

Three weeks after D'Angelo moved in, I received a call from a friend of mine in South Dakota, Deputy Frank Smith. We had worked together on two cases previously and had a good rapport.

I asked, "What's shaking out there in the hinterland?"

"Hey man, thought I would ring you up and tell you the bad news, personally. John Thatcher has been arrested for killing his stepson."

"Damn, that doesn't sound like the John Thatcher I know. There is no way he can be guilty."

"He was alone in the jail watching his stepson Slug on a Sunday afternoon. No one came to visit, and Slug was locked in a cell. Time came to feed him, he was still locked in his cell with a broken neck. I looked at the scene, Matt, and it looks bad for him. The evidence is so strong that we don't think he can beat this. I go to see him every day, and he seems in good spirits. He asked after you. I think he wants you on this to help me."

"There's something amiss in this that you are just not seeing. I know John, and I know he is innocent."

"No choice but to charge him. The South Dakota Department of Criminal Investigation was called in. The forensic evidence is over-whelming. So now he's locked up in Mitchell because we have the jail preserved as a crime scene. He has a good lawyer, but I don't see him beating this. I wish you were here to check this out. Why don't you jump in your car and come out?"

"There's four of us now, two guys, two dogs. You got room?"

"I'll make room, no sweat there. Just make sure you bring your fishing gear and golf clubs for when we get him off," said Frank.

"Okay, but pack in some groceries, I got an eater with me. Should be there tomorrow night."

Putting down the phone, I asked, "D'Angelo, you want to go on a road trip for a couple of weeks?"

"Sure, suppose you can teach me to drive?"

"I don't know. That requires a lot of paperwork. How old are you?"

"Not really sure. Been streeting it for a while. Mom left while I was in the sixth grade. I did the foster home thing for a while, but that really sucks."

"I see. We will be crossing state lines. So, you are eighteen. Do you understand? Anyone asks you, you're eighteen. Far as we both know, you are eighteen, anyway, so it won't be like you're lying. I need your name too, in case we get stopped."

"It was Johnson when I went to school. Been a long time since I heard it though."

"That's good enough for now, but we got to start detecting stuff about you so we can get you a driver's license. We are going to do some fishing and play a little golf along the way."

"Sounds wonderful to me. Never been fishing or golfing, but I have heard of them." He picked up the backpack I gave him and retreated behind the room dividers. I packed my own clothes, carried my suitcase down, then loaded the golf clubs and fishing poles so I wouldn't have to carry them in the morning. With the backseats flat, there is a lot of room in the Explorer.

I showered and shaved early, followed by D'Angelo. We put his bag, the dog beds, and the food into the car. By the time the sun popped high in the morning sky, we pulled through Mac's for breakfast sandwiches and coffee, then continued south to Interstate 80. We turned right and ran from the sun. We stopped every two hours to walk the dogs, use the restrooms, grab some sodas, and off we would go again. I played a steady diet of Otis Redding and Phoebe Snow. Surprisingly I got no complaint from D'Angelo. We turned north toward Sioux City and pulled into a large truck stop to eat. I needed a break. We took some time walking the dogs, and then left them in the car with the engine running and the air conditioner on high. We parked where we could watch the car, figuring they would be safe for a short time. It would take a brave man to tackle a pit bull to steal an old car.

The truck stop had a buffet and the large plates of salad I ate tasted wonderful. D'Angelo's tastes hadn't changed, he went for the pizza and the hot dogs.

We traveled another hour north and west and before we reached Tindale. I crawled from the car, stiff-legged and sore-backed. The dogs and D'Angelo did not seem affected by the long ride.

Frank's house looked the same, to me, when we pulled in a little after seven. The daylight had faded, but I could see the house looked a little less cared for now. Probably it was just that the yard needed mowing, and the hedge next to the sidewalk, was in need of a trim.

Still, when he opened the door, he had a welcoming smile on his face, and he greeted me with a handshake, then a hug. "Good to see you, Matt." He held his hand out to greet D'Angelo. "Nice to meet a friend of Matt's. Not too many say they are a friend to this crusty old fart."

Thunder followed Bogie through the open door into the house. They searched quickly, checking to see if there was any loose food laying around. By the time we had settled in at the kitchen table with a pot of coffee and a bottle of bourbon, the two dogs were curled up next to each other on the couch.

"Let's get the bad news over with first," Frank says. "John got out on bail last night. His wife shot him after he returned home and then killed herself."

"I went over to see him and found John in the bathroom, slumped over in the tub. I assumed he was trying to wash the smell of the jail off. His wife killed him in the shower by emptying John's service pistol into him. She reloaded one shell, undressed, went to bed, pulled the covers up over her head, and pulled the trigger with the gun in her mouth. It was a hell of a mess.

"I figured that she must have believed John killed Slug. She had advanced pancreatic cancer and that causes a lot of pain and can affect the brain. She probably didn't want to live, knowing that her husband had killed her youngest son

"The town is in shock now. Sorrow for the two deaths, both of them were loved, but relief too because they didn't want to see John go through a trial and be convicted of murder. Margo's death is a mercy also, she was in horrible pain. I'm afraid I called you out here on a closed case."

I pulled the cork out of the bottle of bourbon, poured a healthy shot into my coffee, took a long pull, then just looked at Frank for a moment. "Too bad she didn't have the faith in him that we do. I really liked John. A man of few words, but you could believe everything he told you. I refuse to believe he is the killer. As long as I am here anyway, let's look into Slug's killing."

He poured a shot into three glasses, and handed us each one, "Here is to true friends. I am so relieved you came to help, Matt. You too, D'Angelo, it's nice to have you here."

D'Angelo was still choking a little on the bourbon when I interrupted, "Hey Frank, this is off the subject, but D'Angelo is paperless. We'd sure like to get him a driver's license, a social security card, and a fishing license so we can hit the water."

"Fishing license is no problem. Gordon at the hardware store will take my word for him; after all, I'm acting sheriff. Tomorrow I'll ask Rosa to work her magic. See if we can get him papered up."

"You want to see the jail tonight?"

"Let's wait until tomorrow. I'm shot from all the driving. Think I'll hit the sack. Where you putting us?"

"You take the same room. I'll make up the couch for D'Angelo."

I went to take a shower and fifteen minutes later was warm in bed. It turned out my mind wouldn't shut down. I kept revisiting the times I had spent with John.

I knew and trusted John Thatcher. He had never done anything to undermine his straight up honesty. He had been sheriff for over twelve years. He was a stocky, short man with unbounding energy. His whole crew was made better by their confidence in him. He would back them, take the heat off them. He was the one in charge, and the responsibility for the department started and ended with him.

He found me when I was not far from death and hiding from an outlaw motorcycle gang intent on killing me. I'm alive now because Sheriff John was willing to buck the cycle gang on my behalf. He believed that was the right thing to do. That rescue and save happened several years back when John was a well respected officer of the law. He will always be a stand up man in my memory. He had the kindness and bravery to search for me, a stranger to him, when the rest of the world cared not the slightest whether I continued to exist. I finally dozed off, clear set in my mind that John was innocent, and we would prove it.

4

Javase

SHE IS FOURTEEN and fidgeting at her desk. Twisting to look at a clock that is moving agonizingly slowly, crossing and uncrossing her legs, doodling a picture, then scratching it out, glancing again at the clock's hands. Patience has never been Javase's strong trait. She pats her front left pocket making sure her cigarettes are still there. She needs one now but knows she only has a few minutes until this class ends. She can feel her life racing past in this airless, dusty classroom. Mr. Lapour is droning on and on about a poem by Shelley which she had been assigned to read, but Javase never does homework. She knows college is an impossibility. Her stepfather is a deputy. Her mother doesn't work. In a family with three kids, there is never going to be sufficient money for her to attend college. She doubts she will even graduate high school for that matter. These long slow days are all a waste of time. Her future is spread out before her and it looks wonderful. She will be a dancer first, lots of travel, tons of money, exciting times, and men watching her, mesmerized by her skills and enchanted by her beauty. Then she will get a break, and ta da, she will be up on the screen in the movies. Bit parts to start, but she will end up a star. High school is just a waste.

Her skin is a light mocha color that puts her in the out-crowd of popu-
larity. The popular boys keep her lumped together with the Indians,
Mexicans, and other non-white undateable. She keeps her hair shoulder length and curly. It's convenient and inexpensive. Cheap and
thrifty is a big deal in her family life. Her makeup is seldom more
than mascara with a light lipstick. Fully developed, with a body that
draws covert glances and appreciative whistles, she knows she will
not need the breast enhancement surgery several girls in her class
have already had. Her beauty, sexuality, and low vibrant voice are
all the tools she will need to advance through school and eventually
through life.

Tonight she is going to a sleep-over at LeeAnn's house. It's a
break for her from 'clean the house', 'cook dinner', and 'babysit the
kids for a few hours'.

She won't even have another bitter fight with her mother. Each
night not at home is one better day of existence without the parental
battle.

At the bell, she slowly rises and walks to Mr. Lapour's desk. Standing
close to him, she slips on her mantle of overt sexuality and vulnerability.
She asks in a low tone, what the assignment is for the following day. In
her worn tee-shirt and jeans that appear molded to her skin, she knows
Mr. Lapour is not paying as much attention to what she is saying as he
is to her proximity to him. She knows she will pass this class when she
casually rests her hand on his and sees the hair stand up on his arm even
though he quickly pulls back from her touch.

At LeeAnn's house, the five young women play board games and
talk about the boys at school until dinner. LeeAnn's parents had set
up an outdoor cookout in the backyard. Her father prepared his grill,
with plenty of burgers and dogs for everyone. A quiet man, he seldom
speaks to the girls as he flips the food. President of a bank during the
day, he feels ill at ease with all the young women in his backyard. Her
mother, Penny Ann, makes sure everyone has plenty to eat.

"Have you tried the potato salad yet, Javase? I still use my mother's recipe.

I'll write it down for you if you want it."

"Thank you so very much, Mrs. Selvitz." Like she really wanted to get a recipe for potato salad. Anything she threw on the table for her family, they ate. Why work over it?

Later the girls watch horror movies in the living room. That always seemed to be a ritual at sleepovers, but Javase never cares for the moronic stories or cardboard acting in these movies. They just seem so stupid and lame compared to real life. She is more interested in LeeAnn sitting next to her and while reaching for some popcorn, makes sure her arm brushes gently against LeeAnn's chest. Her hand drops innocently into LeeAnn's lap after they all clap at one of the movie scenes. She lets it remain there motionless, certain that LeeAnn is aware of it. She makes the mandatory noise along with others so she will be invited to the next sleep over. It's early the next morning when the girls carry their sleeping bags down to the play room, set up in the basement. Unzipping the bags all the way and spreading them open on the floor, to be used as padding, they pull sheets and blankets over them for warmth. Talk runs on about the movies and who's the cutest boy at school, and which one looks like Jason in the film, soon they begin nodding off. Javase as always, comes to the sleeping area last, making sure she is on the far right side of the group. She hates to be in the middle with no room to move. She is secretly pleased that LeeAnn has arranged to sleep beside her. Javase has rolled onto her right side to sleep, but as the girly noises quiet down to steady breathing, she feels the soft bump of LeeAnn's elbow. It's gentle as if by mistake.

Soon however, a knee moves slowly against her back.

"You sleeping?"

"Mmm," she murmurs, knowing anticipation will build a hotter fire in LeeAnn.

Soon she feels a small hand circling her side, gently pulling her over so she faces LeeAnn, continuing to pull until they embrace. A soft kiss.

"Mmm, okay," she says, "but be as quiet as you can, and this time I'm get to be the guy."

She holds both of LeeAnn's arms pinned over her head with one hand. She first lightly kisses her neck, appreciating the shiver that goes through the girl. Then works her way gently up toward her captive's lips. LeeAnn turns her face to Javase and they kiss. Lightly at first as Javase moves her free hand across the girl's body to gently caress one breast. She forces the eager mouth open with her tongue as she moves her hand slowly lower. LeeAnn's body trembles there in the basement of her parents' house. Javase reaches around, pulling LeeAnn's smaller body over on top, so Javase has her light fragrant blonde hair floating down and brushing her face.

She loves the feeling of LeeAnn's soft sexy hair caressing her face as they kiss deeply.

Later, the two stand outside in the chill night air sharing a cigarette and a beer taken from the cooler in the basement. Javase is always amused when LeeAnn calls these sessions 'learning.' She knows it is just plain sex. It would just be a little different with a man. Men never smell as good and they're always more insistent.

5
The Gambler

AFTER OMELETS AND hash browns, the three of us sit around sipping our coffee. "Nice to be out here with you again, Frank. I love the city, but time out here in a small town is very relaxing. Sure hope we can find the time to play a few rounds of golf while we're here. D'Angelo hasn't tried it yet, but he's up for a challenge. Figure we can show him a lifetime of frustration with just a couple of afternoons."

"You probably forgetting I got the body of an athletic superstar?" says D'Angelo. "I'll try to take it easy on you two, don't want to beat you too bad on the first time out." He picks up his coffee and flops onto the living room sofa. I hear the television come on and hear Drew Carey's voice.

"That would be so kind of you, Superstar. While you're here, learning what the right price is, would you watch the dogs? We'll be gone for a couple of hours. Unless you want to ride along and check out the jail."

"I got no curiosity at all about looking at a jail. Fact is, I spent most of my life trying not to see the inside of a jail. I'll be just fine here."

Frank and I push away from the table. I hear the television shut off, and D'Angelo comes in to sit at the table. He pulls the computer over to him, and it beep, beep, beeps as it's turned on. I look back as we're leaving, and he is sitting in front of the computer, one dog on each side of him with their heads resting each on one foot.   I'm beginning to be a sentimental old fool, but I'll be damned if the three didn't look cute together.

Frank gets into the sheriff's car. "It's only a couple of blocks, but we might as well spend the county's gas money. Besides, it will make this look official. I like to leave this car out where everyone can see it. Keeps the traffic moving slow. They are sure I have my radar going."

We park a half a block up the street from the jail, under a large maple tree, and walk down. Frank is dressed in his full deputy regalia; it must be hot and heavy. I'm wearing athletic shorts and a Cabela's tee shirt. I was a fan of Bermuda shorts, but these new pull on athletic shorts that the kids are wearing, last forever and they are so cool. I've been told I look like a dork in them, but what the fuck do I care what I look like? It's not like I have anyone to impress.

"Why didn't you park in back?"

"Couple of reasons, no entry at the rear. The back door can only be opened by someone inside the building, and the car will be cooler later, sitting in the shade."

"If you can only enter from the front, that should make our job easier. All we gotta do is check the people who walked in the front door. I suppose you already checked the tape?" I ask.

"As if this cheesy little office has the front door taped. By the way, that was one of my suggestions to John. We could have gotten one of those delayed tapes that only come on with motion. It would have knocked $60 a month off the insurance. John presented it at the City Council but they declined. The idea of putting out money runs against the grain for those cheap bastards. They get elected by how much money they don't spend. I suspect they have the cheapest liability insurance they can find on this building. And that's only because there's a law that the building must be covered."

"They're pennywise like most minor politicians. Their primary job is make sure they get re-elected. While it's stupid that they didn't install a motion activated tape, I can understand they must look appealing to their constituency," I say.

"This place is mostly a holding tank for the occasional drunk. With the mental hospital in Yankton and a reservation up in Wagner, we have ended up with several severe alcoholics that frequently pass out on the streets or in the bars. We pick them up and hold them in a cell until two or three in the morning. They are rudely awakened and given a ride back home to sleep it off. Anything serious, we use the facility in Mitchell where they have a proper jail and trained jailers. There is just not much action in this small county."

He stopped in front of the building and began fishing in his pocket for the keys. Pulled out a set. While he sorted out the correct key, I studied the sidewalk. There were a few scuffs showing that at least one person had crossed the street and picked up a little tar on his shoes. He had dragged his feet trying to wipe it off. I stepped into the street and felt the still visible tar.

Frank opened the door, and we entered to the stale captive air. The building was overheated in the morning sun. He blocked the front door open with a worn wooden doorstop, then walked to the AC unit which he clicked on.

"Come on to the back, I'll get the doors open, see if we can get some air moving in here." He unlocked the cell block door with a latch on the office side and propped it open with a chair. The other side of the door required a key to open it. He walked to the rear door. He used his keys on it, then held it open with a brick, obviously left there for that express purpose.

"Hopefully that'll get the air moving."

I looked back at the two barred rooms that comprised the cell block. They were bolted to the front wall and to each other. There was a yard of empty space between the second cell and the far wall. The only natural light came from a small grimy window on the back wall. It too was barred over.

Three industrial strength fluorescent lights blinked on when Frank flicked the switch.

"Delightful place to go slowly crazy," I said.

"Yep," says Frank. "Absolutely dismal."

We returned to the front office, now that the air was becoming breathable. One beat-up wooden desk, with little on it. A black and white television on a small stand, and a rolling chair behind the desk. I sat in the chair. It was a comfortable, twisting, tilting, well-padded chair. There was a toilet door plainly marked toilet in front of the desk.

"So here I am, Sheriff John. I got nowhere else to sit unless I go into a cell. No one can enter that I won't see, even if I am watching the Vike's on television. So let's assume the killer came in the back door."

"Couldn't have," said Frank. "Let me show you."

The lock on the back door can only be opened from the inside with a key. It locked automatically every time the door shut. The outside of the lock was covered over with a welded piece of mental. There was no indication that the metal had been tampered with in any way.

"Which cell was Slug in?"

"The front one."

We examined the cell carefully: the mattress, the pillow, the frame of the bed - nothing.

"Here's something strange, John told me the keys were locked in the cell with Slug. He had to get a broom handle to drag them over to where he could reach them, so he could get into Slug's cell. Only thing I could come up with to explain that, was that they must have fallen out of John's pocket after he had locked the cell. He didn't hear them fall because Slug was probably screaming at him.

"He didn't notice the missing keys until Rosa brought burgers and potato salad for them to eat at six. He used his private keys to get into the cell block. They couldn't wake Slug, so they knew something was very wrong. When they were able to get into the cell, they knew he was dead. John called me, then the coroner.

"See, I know John was just waiting until dark, then he'd have taken Slug home to watch television. They were always friendly to each other. Slug, being a regular fuck-up, had run-ins with John, but it was always professional and they got along pretty good for a step relationship.

"Margo was dying of pancreatic cancer. John and Slug worked together to make sure her last days were as pain free and comfortable as they could make them." I'm sure they both valued and cared for each other because of the common bond they held for Margo. I just refuse to believe John killed him."

"He didn't. The key's the thing that should prove John couldn't have done it. He needed the keys to get back into the front office."

"I did consider that, but I believe John has all the keys on his private ring. So if he didn't have the cell block door key, he might have just used his private key and never thought about it," said Frank.

"Anyone else have extra keys?"

"I don't think they do. Why make a key for a door you very seldom use?"

"I can show you how this was done. I don't know who did it, but we'll get him, don't worry. I know he has a key to that front door, so that should cut the list of suspects down. At least we both know it wasn't John Thatcher.

"Let me show you what happened." I took him to the front door and showed him the tar imprints on the sidewalk. "I believe that had to have been done on Sunday, because people would have stepped in it and spread it out, if it was put there on Monday. On Sunday, few people were walking downtown and that tar hardened in the sun. Someone crossed the street here at a difficult place because he was in a hurry." I took him back into the office. "Here barely inside the door is another patch of it. It could be that John walked across the street for some strange ass reason, but I doubt it. I believe that was laid down by our killer. I think he just got lucky, and he opened that front door with a key while John was in the toilet. I suspect he was prepared to kill Thatcher too. He grabbed the keys from the desk as he walked through, opened the cell block, opened the cell door, got close enough to Slug to kill him quickly. Relocked the cell door, propped the back door open, threw the keys back into the cell, and exited by the back door. He had to be pretty quick and quiet about everything, because John didn't hear him and come to see what was going on. It could be that John was doing a long dump with a paper, but I doubt that because the Vikings were playing. "

"Shee-it," says Frank. "Makes sense the way you lay it out. There's John, Rosa, and me, that have keys. Also, all four deputies. Still, it could be possible someone has made a duplicate, but it would have to have been made in advance, and I don't see anyone just wanting to make a duplicate key for the fun of it.

"Can't see Rosa killing him because she's not strong enough. We both believe John didn't do it, and I will promise you here and now that I didn't do it. That leaves the four deputies. All have the physical prowess, all have keys, and all knew Slug."

"Yuppers," I say. "We got the who pared down to four, now all we need to do is figure out is the why. And we can't do it here. Let's go back to your place and get some coffee."

We relax for a few minutes, eat a sandwich, and pour out a cup of aged black coffee.

"Seems to me that we need to interview the deputies. Do you want to help?" asked Frank.

"Certainly. Do you think they will object to my being there?"

"None of them will object, they all know you're here to help. To object would point a finger at themselves."

"Then set it up, I'll be there. One suggestion: have their wives come in an hour after we interview their husbands. They are all going to say they were at the picnic. Our afternoon will be spent trying to figure out who is lying."

"It will have to be in a few days, my afternoon tomorrow will be spent at the Thatcher's funeral. You and D'Angelo want to come? Probably get to see everyone in town."

I shouted over my shoulder to D'Angelo, "Hey, Young Guy, you want to go to a funeral tomorrow afternoon with me and Frank?"

"Nope, I'm good."

"What time you want me ready?" I asked Frank.

"One o'clock will be good."

"I can be ready by then. If you have a few minutes now, how about telling me about John and Margo?"

Frank leaned back in his chair, took a short drink of his coffee. I watched him closely. This was something that he wanted to say correctly. "I always felt they were doing great. When they met, they were like two drowning souls clutching to each other like a life vest. Margo was taking chemo-therapy for a bad cancer. They didn't talk about it much, but I believe it was pancreatic cancer. John was a caring soul and looked after her carefully. They went dancing often, that country line step shit, and they loved fishing, and pheasant hunting. They were as busy as they could be, considering Margo's illness. Socially they hosted card parties, had friends over often, and of course, church every Sunday.

Margo had three sons. They were all grown, and only the youngest was still at home. As far as I could tell, John was friendly with all three stepsons. The youngest son's real name is James, but he has always been called Sluggo, after the Nancy and Sluggo cartoons. He moved back in with John and Margo so that he could help John with her care. He was devoted to his mother, and seemed to like John.

I knew about him from the time he was a senior in high school. He was short and fast as hell. He made the A-Team just because of his toughness and speed. After high school, he started work in construction. He had a good reputation around this part of the state. He worked hard and put in an honest day. He found work steadily, even if it was only a week here and two weeks there. I remember talking to him at the Nook one day, when he told me he had two job offers and couldn't decide which to take. One job was only for a week, but it paid a thousand. The other job was for two weeks at five hundred a week. He told me he thought he would take the two week job, because it seemed more permanent. That was just his personality. Very likeable when he wasn't drinking.

That said, he was also a stupid fuck-up after a few beers. It seemed at times like he planned ways to irritate people. He would be sitting with friends at a bar, and he would eat the butts in the ashtray, then puke them back up on the table. Guaranteed to start a fight, and Slug always lost. At a restaurant, he would stand outside and knock on the glass until everyone looked, the he would hack up on the window. Probably most of the upstanding people in town disliked him. He had a core of friends who knew and liked him, thinking his antics were funny. Like the day at the picnic when he scooped the food out of the bowls with his hands, then he ran around the park, playing priest, using his beer to bless all the people by splashing beer on them. John always ended up going to get him. Break up the fights, bring him back to Tindale to sober up. He didn't always lock him up, he usually just took him home, and they watched sports together with Margo. That Sunday, John put him in the jail so he wouldn't be accused of favoritism. After all, he had pissed off most of the citizens in town.

As far as I've been able to find, he was honest. And he was brave. Do you know why they had the picnic in the park the day he died?"

"No one ever said."

"They were celebrating Slug the Hero. Two weeks ago he was sitting up on the bluffs of the Missouri down near Springfield. He was probably half drunk since it was six in the evening. Watching the river, he saw two canoes of kids floating downstream. They were having a great time, laughing, shouting at each other. Somehow, they got twisted around and one canoe tipped over. The commotion and grabbing for the other canoe, got it tipped over also. It doesn't take much to tip a canoe. Being kids, some of them tried to swim to shore, rather than just hold on to the canoes. They were unable to make it, and they were all terrified.

Sluggo, the fuck up, took a short run, jumped off the bluff, and with blind luck landed in water deep enough that he didn't break his neck. He swam to the canoes, helped the kids back in, then pushed them in to shore. Two needed resuscitation. He showed the oldest girl how to do it, while he worked on the other. Both kids pulled through. He saved the lives of those two for sure, probably saved all of them. Never thought about himself at all, the kids were in danger and he flew into action. Strange kind of guy, wasn't he? That is why he had people who really liked him. He might irritate you, but he was still the guy who came through to save your child in an emergency. You just never knew what he would do next."

"Well, Frank, someone here hated him or feared him. They thought he was going to do something that would jeopardize them. That is a reason they had to silence him."

Later that evening, in the cool of the twilight, I take out a fishing rod with an open faced reel for D'Angelo. At the kitchen table, under the lights, I demonstrate how it works, explain the drag setting and its use to him. Now comes the hard part, learning to tie knots every fisherman has to know. I use the improved cinch knot for almost everything. With his nimble fingers, he learns it in minutes. We take the rod and reel out to Frank's backyard, and D'Angelo begins casting. He is very polite, but I can feel his superior attitude that this is easy stuff. His first cast leaves the weight laying on the ground behind him; he took his finger off the line too soon. Second cast lands ten feet in front of us; he held it too long. Now concentrating hard, he tries again, forgetting to pull his arm back and the line ties into a knot on the end of the pole.

"D'Angelo, it can be frustrating, but take your time and think about each step. Soon it will be like second nature to you."

By the fifth cast, he has the hang of it. At least, good enough to begin fishing.

We have to wait until later in the morning, the next day. Frank rides down to the hardware store with us and vouches for us so we can get licenses. They also sell bait there, and we get a couple of dozen worms. I drive down to Memorial Park, and pull the Explorer in at the end of a row of six cars. We are the only vehicle that doesn't have a boat trailer attached. There is no one else at the park that I can see.

We are at least two blocks down from the double decker bridge that is part of Highway 80, The Pan American Roadway. Before President Eisenhower started building the interstate road system, this had been one of the major highways in America: stretching from Canada, through the United States, and down into South America. The double decker is still an impressive structure, although now it is used more like a local bridge connecting South Dakota to Nebraska.

The shoreline is dotted with huge cottonwoods moving with every gentle breeze. Their leaves flash silver and green as the early morning sun glints through them. The far end of the park is hidden by a slight bend in the river bank.

D'Angelo and I walk down to the rocks next to the dock and begin rigging our rods. When we are ready, we head down to the boat dock on the mighty Missouri, which has a steady four to five mile an hour current. The depth along the shore we are fishing runs from 10 to 15 feet deep. As with all rivers, there is debris float-ing downstream, that adds to the roots, rocks, and assorted crap embedded in the river's bed, providing unlimited snags designed to irritate the fishermen. There are several large companies and many small businesses that survive on providing hooks, sinkers, and a wide assortment of gear with the promise of catching fish, but also carrying the certainty that they will snag something and be lost, another sacrifice to the river bottom. The Missouri river fish are attracted to moving bait, so the successful angler will keep his line moving downstream, bouncing the bait off the bottom. He who catches more Bigmouth Bass, also catches more Log Bass. So the ability to tie knots on the shoreline and in the dark rapidly, reattaching hooks and sinkers, is a must.

D'Angelo has lost two complete rigs and is working his third downstream with a fat night crawler as bait, when he gets his first strike. His pole bends almost in half. It must be a good sized fish.

"Keep the tip up, then set the hook," I tell him. He's fighting the fish hard. Walking much too close to the edge of the dock, I'm hoping he won't fall in with the excitement of the catch.

"I'll get the net," I tell him. "You're doing good, but watch out for the wet part of the dock, it's slippery."

There is a lot of splashing, and runs, and recovery, but finally, D'Angelo gets a large carp near the dock, and I net him. I heft him several times, "Feels like a fifteen pounder to me. Damn nice fish, D'Angelo." I unhook the fish, put it in the bottom of the cooler and cover it with ice. Usually I wouldn't keep a carp, but it's D'Angelo's first and we'll clean and eat it. He's not saying much, but I can see he's standing a little taller, chest puffed out just a bit.

D'Angelo notices a young girl standing back by the trees watching Matt beginning to work his fly in the rapidly moving water. She is deep into the shadows of the cottonwoods, but he can still make out through the large shirt she wears and the tight jeans she has painted on, that she is well developed and almost as tall as him. His breath is catching slightly in his throat, and he turns back to the river. He reels in, checks his bait, then casts back out, upstream and away from Matt. He looks back for another quick glance. She has raven black hair. Her face is light mocha and shows the clean smooth lines of youth. Her eyes are large and widespread with dark pupils which seem to absorb some of him when she looks at him. He finds he is having trouble breathing.

She is watching Matt work his fly line. He is casting out about thirty yards, letting the current take his fly downstream. When it begin swirling in toward the shore, he starts a slow retrieval.

"Good morning." He is watching his fly intently, and D'Angelo wonders how he knew she was there.

"Good morning, yourself," she says, coming closer to watch him fish. "How come you don't use any bait?"

"I am fly fishing. It's something old guys do. I have a tiny artificial fly tied onto the end of my line. That's what you would call my bait. It should be good until my line breaks. When I recast it, the air dries it and it continues to float." Something big hits my Royal Coachman right then and almost tears the rod out of my hand. I have been paying attention to the girl, not the fly. I manage to get my tip up and begin playing the fish as he takes out more line before I can slow him up. I only use a four pound tippet, so I can't horse him or he will snap the line and be gone. He is a dasher, fast and powerful, but after several minutes, I can feel him weaken and start to prepare him for the net.

I am standing on a narrow dock, and my hand net had been left on the grass at the edge of the dock.

"Sweetheart," I ask, "would you bring me that net? I want to get a look at him before I let him go."

"Sure," she nimbly picks up the net and runs it out to me.

"Do you want to net him?" I ask.

"Heck yes."

"Okay, just dip the net in the water first so it gets wet. There is less chance of hurting him with a wet net. That way we can let him go to be caught again."

She kneels on the edge of the dock, dips the net in the water, and waits until he swims close to the dock. She neatly picks the fish up and holds it high.

"Awesome," she yells, holding the net high above her head with her right hand. "It's gorgeous, look at the size of him."

"Largemouth Bass," I say. "Nice fish. Hold him over here, and I'll take the hook out. I use the forceps to pop the hook out of his lip. An aggressive fish like the Largemouth seldom swallows the fly, he is usually hooked by just the lip and easy to release unharmed. This bad boy weighs in at about six pounds. Nice fish.

"Do you ever eat them?"

"Oh sure, it's good table fare, but we are staying at a friend's house and have no way to cook him."

"If you're going to release him, can I have him? He looks large enough to feed my whole family."

"Absolutely," I say. I kill him with a blow to the head, remove his head, and fillet him there on the dock. He dresses out with what feels like three solid pounds of muscle.

D'Angelo surprises me by saying, "If you want it, you can take my fish too."

"Certainly, my family loves fish." She flashes a brilliant smile at him.

I say, "Your fish is pretty heavy D'Angelo, you might want to help her carry it home."

They put the bass fillets on the ice and walk off, each carrying a handle on the cooler.

"Thanks again," the girl shouts as she walks away.

I still feel bad about killing the fish. That was a superb bass.

When D'Angelo returns, we head back to Frank's for breakfast. Give the dogs a good half hour walk. I have to return to get ready for the funeral. This is going to be jeans and a pullover for me. I suspect I will be severely underdressed, but I wasn't family, only a casual friend, and I doubt my dress will be noticed.

6
The Funeral

THE FUNERAL FOR John and Margo is being held at the Church of Christ the Savior. A small newly built stone building, it sits on an empty lot on the north edge of the town. People are standing around, I notice a few are entering the building. I stay outside with Frank talking. He leads me through the crowd and introduces me to his deputies. I am surprised that I know one, Wyatt Daniels. He had been three years ahead of me in high school. They are dressed in full uniform.

A tall deputy named Johnson is the most congenial, he comes over to shake my hand.

"Good day to you, Matt. I think you're the man who gave my daughter, Javase, that great fish this morning. So nice of you. We are looking forward to having it tonight."

"You have a very nice daughter. She's a sweet girl. Hope you love the fish."

"She is my treasure. Want to come over and meet some more people? My family is right over here."

I followed him, after telling Frank I would be right back.

"This is my wife, Silvia."

I extend my hand, "Nice to meet you Silvia, I'm Matt Smith."

"You met Javase this morning," he said, pointing to her. She responds with a nod of her head. "This is my son, Aaron, and my youngest daughter, Madison."

All three kids are dressed in their Sunday clothes. Standing in the afternoon sun they look uncomfortable. The kids are not that interested in meeting me, but I have a thick hide. My pride is unaffected.

Deputy Johnson walks with me through the crowd and introduces me to another five or six couples. I remember the first couple, Al and Janet Cobb. They had sponsored a bereavement group ever since they lost their son Jacob in Iraq. They live just north of town. The next couple is Lana and Reynard Appledorn, after that the names run together quickly. As we walk, everyone has a kind word or backslap for Deputy Johnson, seems he is a well-liked person.

The crowd had begun to move into the church and by the time I went in, it was mostly full. I sat near the back of the church next to an older lady smelling of stored clothing. Next to her was a florid faced man with white hair, hanging too long down the sides of his head. Pretty much bald on top. He leaned over to shake my hand.

"I'm Sam Kelley. You called me last year when you saw my gates were left open, saved me a ton of trouble with those cattle of mine. They love to wander. If you hadn't called, they'd have been all over the county."

"Nice to meet you, Mr. Kelley." I sat back for a moment, thinking of his abandoned farmhouse just out of town where I noticed the open gates. Then an idea presented itself. I leaned forward to talk to him again. "Mr. Kelley, is that house still empty?"

"Yes, more houses than people in this county."

"Would you consider renting it to me? I need a separate mailing address, it seems like the perfect place."

"Certainly, that place has great water and a deep well. Turn on the electricity and it's ready to go. Call me tomorrow and we'll talk. You'll love that place."

"I'm booked tomorrow. How about if I give you $100 now? Just mail me the keys and receipt in the mail to the house."

"Done," he said, and I gave him the money.

Pastor John led the funeral service, gave an excellent homily, spoke well of his two good friends John and Margo, and ended with 'Amazing Grace'.

I rode out to the cemetery with Frank. I really hadn't planned to, but once you get wrapped in the arms of a ceremony, it can be difficult to break away without showing disrespect.

7
Matt

BY SIX-THIRTY THE next morning after a restless night's sleep, I woke up Frank. "Can we swing by John's house? I would like to get a look at the death scene."

"Give me a minute to get dressed." He shouted to me. I heard him bumping and banging around some, and finally he emerged fully dressed. "Want to walk?" He asked me.

It was a short three block walk to the large two story house with a traditional picket fence across the front and a small sidewalk leading to the front door.

"No yellow tape?" I questioned.

"It was ruled a murder suicide by the coroner and is no longer a crime scene. The sons will be coming to clean it out and list it for sale, probably soon after the funeral."

We walked around to the back of the house which butted up against a cornfield.

"Nice to have the nothing behind your house, that would surely keep the noise down," I said. There was an overhanging screened-in back porch with a large welcome sign before the door. Frank lifted the rug, took out a key, and opened the door.

"Thatcher wasn't much on high security."

The floor was piled high with jumbled boots and old shoes. Inside the door, there was an open closet hung with jackets and coats. Just beyond the closet was the kitchen. Frank went to the sink, opened his thermos, took down a couple of cups, and poured. It was kind of chilly in the empty house, and the warm cups felt good in our hands. I started to wander, but Frank pulled a bag out of his coat pocket and opened it on the table. "A couple of pastries will help sharpen our minds," he said.

Indeed, the apple fritter I bit into tasted great and I'm sure the excessive sugar intake did help me focus.

Frank led me to the door of the kitchen, "Here's where we found John. He was taking a shower. His clothing was thrown over a kitchen chair. I figured he wanted to get the stink of the jail off."

"That seems reasonable to me," I said. "Was the water still running when you arrived?"

"Yes, he had a head full of shampoo. You can see where the bullets exited his body and chipped the tiles. I think he must have been dead almost instantly. Otherwise, he would have turned and been facing the door. Maybe trying to get out of the shower."

"Where did Margo die?"

Frank led me into the living room and opened a door off to his right. "This was their bedroom. The last six months, Margo had been too sick to climb the stairs, so John converted this extra room to a bedroom. Her body was on the far side of the bed. She was covered over with blankets, and her head was resting on the pillow. When I first came in, I didn't see her. Then I noticed the blood above the headboard. She had pulled the blankets up over her head. I'm think she probably wanted quiet and warmth at the end."

"Was she dressed?"

"She was wearing only a nightgown."

"Has anything been moved in here?" I asked. "Other than John's clothes, which I can see have been moved onto the bed."

"No, nothing I can see anyway. Why?"

"Because it doesn't hold up as a murder-suicide. With no hard proof to give you, I can still say that what you have here is a double homicide."

"What do you see that convinced you of that?"

"John was arrested on Sunday. Margo had to be up and dressed. If she had been too sick to get up, Thatcher would have stayed here tending to her, not down at the jail. He would have called you in to watch the prisoner as you were the only one without a family at the park, except Wyatt, and he was entertaining. You're probably pretty lucky in that Frank, because the killer would have shot you where you sat when he walked in. Margo had to be well enough to get dressed and eat breakfast with John, and she would have made something to eat later on Sunday and then again on Monday. Still the kitchen is immaculate. The dishes have been all washed and put away, the garbage has been emptied, and a new bag has been put in. In her bedroom, there are no clothes, the hamper is empty. What happened to her clothes? I have a hard time believing anyone would have spent time doing dishes and laundry, when they were thinking about offing themselves.

"If on the other hand, she decided to kill him in the morning, she may have gone into the kitchen in her nightgown, but she would have worn slippers. The cold wood floor in the living room and the hard tile in the kitchen, would have been too uncomfortable. She would have worn something on her feet. There was nothing by the side of her bed and I don't think she would have put them away before she crawled into bed to kill herself.

"Margo would have put four rounds into John and then the fifth into her mouth. There is no way she would have walked back to their bed to commit suicide. This is a carefully orchestrated murder from what I see.

"I think the killer knew Margo. He probably came carrying a fruit basket or flowers. Margo would have welcomed him in. He probably talked for a few minutes and when she turned from him, he grabbed her from the back and suffocated her. Then stripped her clothes off, put them in the garbage, carried her body into the bedroom, put her nightgown on her, and tucked her into bed. He shot her there putting the gun under her chin and shot up through the top of her head, disguising any marks of injury. He probably muffled the sound with pillows, then he covered her up, so John wouldn't notice her if he looked in the bedroom.

"Reloading John's pistol, he changed the garbage bags, taking away her clothes, whatever the present was he brought, and the pillows. He put the garbage bag in the bedroom, where he stood and waited for John to come home. If John had walked into the bedroom, he would have died there. That John would go first to take a shower was knowledge the killer had from watching or knowing other prisoners. The garbage bag was probably put in the can out back and hauled away the next day. I would say it's almost a perfect double murder."

"Christ, Matt. You've got some imagination. Maybe Margo didn't mind walking on bare floors. Given that, your whole case falls through."

"Could be, but if I'm right, we have a very cunning killer to deal with here. I say we treat this as double murder so we keep in mind how ruthless this man is. I believe you could prove it, if you want to delve further into it."

"What are you thinking?"

"John was arrested at the Mitchell jail, so his service pistol would have been impounded there. If they had his pistol until he was released, and my supposition is correct, he would have had to shoot Margo with a different gun. If you take the bullet out of that wall above the bed, you could have forensics compare them at Pierre."

Frank opened his Buck knife, attacked the wall, and held up the bullet. "We'll know within the week."

My night was spent chasing John and Margo through a long maze with an elusive prey managing to stay just ahead of me. I tried to grasp it, but it slipped through my fingers so easily. I woke at 3 a.m. staring at the ceiling. I need to develop my questions. If I can get the right question, I can force an answer. It will have to be one beautiful set of questions. I hope Frank can come up with something brilliant.

Frank had a meeting early that morning, so I ran D'Angelo down to the park for a few hours of fishing. I watched him work his bait. I hadn't brought my own rod because I wanted to think. The immensity of the Missouri rolling down was settling for me. Somehow, I think better watching water. Also satisfying to see D'Angelo absorbed so totally in fishing. Frank's big news when he returned was that he is now the acting sheriff until the next election. The City Council didn't want to spend the money for a one year election.

We have two hours until the deputies show up for the interviews. Frank went about preparing for the interviews in a surprisingly officious manner. I was used to him not acting like the sheriff, but the mantle of the office settled gently around him as the hour for interviews neared. There was a fresh pot of coffee, and the tiny refrigerator held bottled water and soft drinks.

Right at one o'clock on the button, he called in Deputy Steve Anders and his wife Elizabeth. Frank and I had discussed calling husbands and wives in separately, but it seemed to us that the interviews would be dragged out much longer with little chance for significant differences in their stories.

Frank began the interview by asking if they minded me being in the room.

"Not at all," said Anders. "I'm willing to help in any way I can to clear Sheriff Thatcher's name, but I also have to say, I feel it's an excessive waste of time when DCI has already completed their investigation, indicating that Thatcher was the perpetrator of the crime." He said it in a thoroughly impersonal matter, as if it was outside his range of care, and it was up to Frank to waste the time if he so chose.

"Duly noted," said Frank. "You are correct about DCI, but a murder in my county, does make the investigation my business. The investigation is currently being conducted under joint jurisdictions. Do you understand?"

"Yes," he replied, but his eyes and the set of his jaw showed he felt this was still a waste of time that a better acting sheriff would not indulge in.

"Do you have a key to the jail?" asked Frank.

"Sure, Thatcher gave it to me when I signed on with the county."

"Can I see it, please?" Anders handed it to him. Frank examined it closely, then copied the number of the key on the pad of yellow paper before him and handed the key back to Anders.

"Have you ever made a duplicate of it, or loaned it to anyone else?" "No. I keep it on me all the time except when I'm at home. There I keep my keys locked up in my bed stand."

"That's great," said Frank. "My next question is for both you and Elizabeth. It concerns the Sunday that Slug was killed. Where were you, and who were you with during the time from eleven in the morning until three in the afternoon?"

Elizabeth answered for both of them, "We were together getting ready for the picnic, then all four of us walked to the park together. Steve carried the cooler, kids brought the lawn chairs, and I carried the brats," said Liz. "We arrived just as Sluggo was escorted away to the jail. That poor man, he always seems to do the wrong thing in the wrong place. He must have been a real handful for Margo. We sat and talked to people, ate great food, spent some time with Dan, Silvia and their kids, then about one-thirty, Steve and the kids went to play softball. I helped clean up and stack the tables. Around three we all headed on back to the house. Just a nice quiet afternoon with beautiful weather."

"Thanks," said Frank, turning to me, "Any questions, Matt?"

"Yes. Elizabeth, from what you just told us, you didn't see Steve from one-thirty until three. Is that correct?"

"Well, he was only half a block away at the ball diamond with the girls. I didn't have my eyes on him every second, but I looked over several times and saw him there. It would have been impossible for him to leave without me or the kids noticing."

"Steve, where were you when Sheriff Thatcher came back from Mitchell? I believe that was at three o'clock Monday afternoon."

"I drove him back from Mitchell. Let him off at his front door, watched until he walked inside, then I reported back to Frank at three-thirty."

"Have you always lived here in South Dakota, Steve?"

" Pretty much, born and raised in Mitchell. Elizabeth and I fell in love and got married right after high school, then I went to the university in Ames, Iowa. Once I graduated, we moved back here for this job."

"Do you really lock your keys in your bed stand every night? Seems a little excessive to me."

"I try to, but they are always in the drawer, so they are still safe."

"One more question, what do you carry for a back-up?"

"I have a .25 cal. Beretta in an ankle holster."

"Thanks, Deputy Anders, that's all I have."

He stood up, "Anything else, Frank?"

"Nope, thanks for coming in to help. If you remember anything else, please let me know."

After Anders left, Frank turned to me, "I didn't see anything there, did you?"

"Jesus, Frank, that was just the first guy and he had enough holes in his story to have easily killed all three people. Plus, it sounded to me like someone is politicking to kick you out and take over as acting sheriff."

The next interview was with Dan and Silvia Johnson. Dan is six foot, four inches tall, weighs 220 lbs., and is a gregarious friendly man that everyone in town knows and seems to like. Silvia is also tall, six-two, about 200 lbs. with beautiful brown eyes and an engaging smile.

Frank again asked if they minded me being present at the interview. When Dan began the 'already been completed by DCI spiel', I interrupted him half-way through.

"Dan, we've met and talked before. You seem to be on top of everything popping in town. What's all this about DCI? I can't believe you really give a damn how Frank spends his time. Can you tell us where this wasting time crap comes from?"

"Can't rat on a fellow officer. I will say that I think the deputy who started it, has an uncle on the City Council, and would like to have Frank given the boot and get the appointment himself. Burns is the guy you have to watch on the Council. Don't mention my name in this. If you do, I'll deny it."

He was at the picnic with his wife, Silvia, and his three kids. They were together all afternoon, throwing Frisbees and just enjoying themselves. At three o'clock, Monday afternoon, he had been home making lasagna for his family's dinner.

He'd been living in Des Plaines, Illinois, working as a used car salesman. He sold a car to Silvia, then two months later they were married. He had gone to high school in Peoria and attended the University of Western Illinois in Macomb. A highway patrol friend of his told him about the posting in Tindale. Small town South Dakota seemed like a great place to raise kids. After talking it over with his wife, he had applied for the job and was very happy that Tindale had turned out to be such a great place. He didn't carry a back-up gun as there was little real crime here.

Wyatt Daniels, the third deputy, was part time. He had dressed casually, the only one to wear boots and jeans. He was six feet tall, weighed 180 lbs., and at age 58, was the oldest of the deputies. He had spent time at the picnic with his girlfriend, Mona. They had lived together for several years. On Sunday, he had brought his guitar after lunch and had played some old tunes for a sing-a-long. He didn't have a back-up piece. He had spent most of that Tuesday working on the motor of a Piper Cub, for a friend of his. He'd had quite a life. His mother was a full-blooded Cherokee Indian. He was an airplane mechanic. He had moved around a lot, mostly staying in the mid-west, he graduated from the public high school in Emmetsburg, Iowa, but had spent two years in Canada, keeping an outfitter's planes fly-ing. Tired of the intense cold, he had taken a part-time job at the post office in Tindale. When the deputy saw a job had opened up, he thought it would be a good fit. He never drank alcohol because of his heritage. He played his guitar frequently at one of the local bars, got paid in sandwiches and Cokes. He carried a .380 cal. Sig Sauer as a back-up.

The last deputy is Larry Temple, a shorter guy with black hair just starting to gray at the edges. Immaculate uniform and spit shined shoes. He smells of gun oil. His back-up piece is a Sig .38 cal. He's been married for twenty-six years, his wife's name is Sandra, they were married in their second year at USD. His two children are out of the house; one is still in school, the other is married and living in Sioux Falls. He and his wife had enjoyed the food at the picnic, then he joined the members of the horse shoe league in an informal tournament. He had come in third. On Tuesday he had been fishing from early afternoon until dark at Lewis and Clark Lake. His boat is harbored there and the times the boat is in use is logged out and then back in.

He had been born and raised in Vermillion, where he went to USD. He had never lived outside of South Dakota, except for a short stay in Bemidji, Minnesota. That was for his first job in law enforcement. As soon as he could, he had returned to South Dakota. Minnesota winters were brutal.

Now that the deputies are finished, Frank and I each take out a Diet Coke and look at each other.

"Damned if I learned anything from all that," I say. "I would elimi-nate Wyatt, because he was the center of attention with his guitar. Other than that I've nothing. The other three could have slipped off for ten minutes and never been noticed. You pick anything else out?"

"Shit no, I've totally convinced myself that I am no sleuth. If Hercule Poirot had been here, he'd have asked two or three more questions and had the murder all tied up. Everything I ask, I already know the answer to. I certainly haven't turned up anything incriminating."

"What say we go back down to Memorial and sniff around?" We drove to the park and sat in the car next to the ball diamond.

"This is the furthest away from the picnic that any of them reported being. Note the time on your watch. We'll walk to the jail, wait there for two minutes, and walk back. See how long they would have had to have been away and still kill Sluggo at the jail. I calculate the killer took two minutes inside with Sluggo." We walked at an average pace, figuring the killer would not want to appear to be in a hurry. It took exactly four minutes forty seconds. From the back door of the jail, it took twenty-five seconds longer. The killer had been gone right at twelve minutes. Not an unreasonable time for any of them to be gone and not be missed.

8
The Gambler

I SPENT SEVERAL hours going over the answers in my mind. Somewhere in all this, a murderer lies hidden with an easy going camouflage that has him buried in folds of married, small town life. I walk out into the night, light a cigar, and go for a short walk beneath the brilliance of the western stars, trying to clear my head. I've been bombarded with too much information. But how do I cross out the extraneous crap? I walk the five blocks down to the Missouri and sit on the dock watching the water flow. The answer is locked in Sluggo's death. What did he know or see that required him to be killed? While wild thoughts and theories swirl, I begin the walk back to Frank's. A long night of sleep may clear my head of mist.

I notice Chick's, one of the town's bars, is still open, and I go in for a beer. Sleep can wait another hour. Six customers on a Tuesday night, busy night for a local bar. The distinct smell of stale beer and cigarette smoke meld together in an atmosphere made acceptable by the presence of cold beer. There is a woman bartender working tonight. The place looks much better than the last time I was here. Now it has tables and chairs spread out across the floor. The whole place has been painted and a large mirror hangs the length of the bar. A rainbow of neon signs advertising beer is draped over much of the mirror. The last time I'd been in here, the place was painted black. The bartender was a surly bastard named Twho had tried to have me killed. The bar stools then were rickety uneven seats that no one was brave enough to sit on. Everything looks much nicer tonight. Including the lady tending bar. She looks to be pushing forty, and is very cute with short brown hair.

Since my wife's death, I've not been a hermit. After all, the equipment still works, and my eyes still naturally roam to an attractive woman. From what I know about men it's that as long as he is alive, a man always looks.

My trouble is that I have not been very lucky with the women I've been drawn to. The first lady I started a relationship with tried to kill me. The second left me for my brother-in-law while I was hospitalized. I can understand the woman wanting to kill me, but to leave me for that pig-eyed little turkey-neck, still frosts my gizzard. But I'm not dead yet, and that is one cute lady bartender.

Four men are sitting at the bar, watching the television set, cheering for one of the baseball teams playing. They have a good stock of empty bottles sitting on the bar before them. Two younger men are playing darts at the far wall.

New bartender looks at me. "Bud," I say, "no glass."

"No glass," she snorts. "I like that."

She is wearing a plain blue tee covered by bib overalls. They fit her nicely, showing their age by the wear on her knees and butt. Nice looking butt. She looks faintly familiar to me. She digs around in the coolers, comes up with a beer, returns to me and sets the bottle naked on the bar. Apparently they haven't upgraded to coasters.

"You look familiar to me, beautiful. Didn't you used to ride with the motorcycle gang that hung here?"

"You realize don't you, that calling me beautiful is considered a sexist remark?"

"I'm too old to be politically correct, sweetheart, and I do apologize if I have insulted you."

"I'm not insulted. I like a cute dirty old man hanging around and hitting on me," she says with a laugh. "But to answer your question, I did ride with them, part of the stupidity of youth."

"That has to be a tough life," I say, hoping to keep the conversation going.

"I had to be an imbecile to stay with them as long as I did. But my old man rode with them and I stayed with him. It gets to be like an indoctrination. They control everything. You ride when they want to, you cook when they want food, you clean when they say it's dirty. I was like a slave. Still they ruled the county. I was young and crazy. Money rolled in, parties seemed to never stop, and the sex was frequent and rough. I was on top of the world. We all believed we would be part of history, as the start of a motorcycle nation. I never thought of myself as other than a member of the gang, but that is what I was, and by the time you want to get out, you can't. There was nowhere I could go. I couldn't get away. What seems great at eighteen ain't so grand at twenty- eight. They were so big and strong. Ha. It was an angry old man who took them down. One determined old guy. Thank God for him. Because of him, I am my own person."

The phone rings and she hurries to the other end of the bar to answer it. She notes down something on a pad by the phone. I watch her walk down the bar, her legs seem to go on forever. Celibacy, I think, is highly overrated, and in my sad state of affairs it's been over a year. My trouble is my head because I know sexual encounters always carry an emotional element.

She resupplies the baseball crowd with four fresh beers. The phone rings again, and once again she makes a notation on the pad.

I finish my beer and hold it up. She digs around again in the cooler and brings me another Bud.

"Just so you know. I recognized you when you came in."

"I thought you had. Any hard feeling?"

"Hell, no. Glad to be shed of them losers. By the way, one of the guys playing darts called someone when you came in. I would watch them if I was you. This place ain't exactly church."

"Thanks for the heads up. You take bets in here?"

"Just sports. Twinks play Yanks tomorrow so lot of action tonight."

"I'd probably go with the Yankees. Can you put down two hundred for me on the Yanks?"

"I will, but this is the first time we've met. I'll need the money up front. I'll need a tag for you and vig is ten percent."

I give her two bills, "My tag is Bogie."

The phone rings again, and she is off. I watch her walk down the bar moving with a beautiful feminine strut. I glance back at the dart players, and they are approaching me slowly. These are some corn fed country boys with muscles bulging under faded plaid shirts. Work boots and jeans complete their drinking on the town ensemble. They look like gym rats, muscles developed by lifting weights, not actual work. Strength works great for confidence, but speed is usually the essential factor in a fight. Hit first, hit fast, and make the blows count. What I have to avoid is going down where they can grind and pound me down.

Usually in a fight, if there are two guys, especially when the two have been put up for the job, one is the leader and the other is not so enthusiastic. This time it's the smaller guy that's all mouth.

"Lots of guys think I'm a mouthy asshole. Would you believe that?"

"I believe it. I just met you and I think you're an asshole already."

"Hey, that's pretty funny." He turned back to look at the other man. "Don't you think that's funny?"

Big guy doesn't say anything.

"Well, anyway funny guy, what I'm trying to tell you is I can be mouthy, because my brother kicks the shit out of anyone who gives me trouble."

"Do you only get mouthy to little girls and old men? Doesn't look to be a match for much more than that."

"Damn, you got a mouth on you. You oughta keep quiet until I say something to make you mad. Otherwise, he's just going to beat you senseless for no reason."

"I'm sure you'll keep on until he gets hurts bad for no good reason. Then when he's lying there bleeding, you'll be able to help him home."

"Heard you say you were one of them piss ant Yankee fans."

"Is this the part in the conversation where you work at annoying me?"

The bigger guy in back, pushed the other guy out of his way.

"Don't matter anymore, you irritated me, you big city jerk." He is a younger man, maybe twenty-eight to thirty. He has the build of an ex-football player, complete with the fat belly. I'm unsure why he is trying to start a fight with me, but his whole attitude is one of aggression. I look over at him casually. His brother has now moved to stand by his side. Not too worried about Big Mouth, he would only be a factor if I went down.

"Son, you probably think you're safe giving me this excess lip. Perhaps you've had a little luck bullying old people and girl scouts, but let me warn you now. I'm not worried by your size or youth. I'm thinking you'd look good laying out back of the bar bleeding."

The lack of open space worries me, and I step forward to clear the bar stools. They are too easy to trip over. Also, by stepping forward, they no longer believe they are in total control. Probably end up getting me killed some day, but I'm still not backing up.

The front guy asks, "You want to take this outside?"

"Your choice. The floor in here will be easier on your face when you land, the macadam outside will be much rougher. You're the one whose face will be smashed by it, so you get to choose."

"You think you're pretty smart, don't you?"

"That's a big difference between you and me. I can hink, you never did get the thinking or smart part of anything. So what's it going to be: zip and stay or lip and bleed?" He looks like he wants to drag out the insults and is perhaps more intent on establishing his rep here for the people in the bar, than in fighting. I probably should just ignore him, but he will probably keep pushing until I have to fight anyway.

"Why you mouthy old goat," is all he gets out before I hit him with a short right. My fist lands just under his nose, driving it upward. As I expected, his friend backs off a step.

"Yaaghh," grunts Young and Stupid as blood shoots out. A quick left to his ribs right over his liver puts him on the floor, face down as predicted.

"You made a good choice. The parking lot would have left scars on your face."

He rolls over to a sitting position, looks at me while he measures the amount of damage done. He begins to rise slowly, holding on to a bar stool for balance. I hope he is finished with fighting. But no, this is a slow learner and he launches himself at me with his arms spread wide in an attempt to wrap his arms around me. I go to one knee and punch under his reach. He comes to a sudden stop as I hit him in the throat with another right. My fingers are half extended leaving the knuckles sharp and hard to dig deeply into soft tissues. His hands move from almost around me to holding his throat. His knees buckle and he goes down like cow flop on a hot day. His head barks solidly on the worn dirty floor boards, then jerks backward rapidly as his face finds the edge of my boot. I shouldn't have kicked him, but now he will have a nice scar to tell his children about.

His friend has not reacted during the little fracas. The bartender has come up behind me and her hands are below the bar.

I turn my head toward her slightly. "You part of this?"

"Nope," she says. "You got it under control." I turn back to Slim. "Why not help your brother here get home? Seems he's had a little too much to drink and fell off his stool."

As Slim helps his buddy out the door, I finish my beer and order another. My heart is still thundering in my chest. I'm too old for fisti-cuffs with younger men.

"Sure you want to hang around this dump drinking a beer, or would you consider walking a lady home? I'll have a nice cold beer for you there."

"Are you worried that they'll come back?"

"Not with you in here, Tiger."

"Well, darling, I would be proud to walk you home."

"Time to go guys. Bar's closed," she shouts. She turns off the television and despite their grumbling, shoos them out the door and locks it. I slip two quarters in the jukebox as she walks toward the door. She turns back just as the first strains of the music starts and she melts neatly into my arms. It's an oldie, "Ebb Tide". Perfect music for the first slow dance. She moves gracefully, making it a most enjoyable dance.

"Thanks for the dance, now let's get out of here before someone starts knocking on the door."

She turns off all the lights, except the neon signs, leads me to the back door and locks it behind us. It's another beautiful cool night, and we walk quietly for a few blocks. I wonder how big a cookie will be left on my hard drive if this works out good.

"I hope you don't get into trouble over closing early."

"Don't worry too much darling, I own the place. Funny story that. The Servants, idiots that they were, put two of their older members down as owners figuring that as one left or died, they would just put another name on the deed. Like I said, they thought they were for-ever. Then both of the owners die in the James River on the same night. Fools should have never gone swimming at night, especially when there was an angry man with a knife swimming also. What they didn't think of was that my old man and me got married by Elvis in Las Vegas. My guy loved Elvis. When the smoke all cleared, I owned the bar. As you see, you are my hero and benefactor."

Lovely Lovely turns up a walkway to a small two story frame house, unlocks the door and invites me in. She leads the way into the kitchen by turning lights on and off, opens the fridge and pulls out two beers, handing me one. Picking up a small remote, she pushes a button and Sarah Vaughn's sultry voice comes on, singing about Vermont. Beautiful steps into my arms again. The warmth and softness of her in my arms is intoxicating. She's a perfect size and lays her head against my chest as we move together to Sarah's incredible voice. Somewhere in the middle of "Broken Hearted Melody" we kiss. He lips are firm and she kisses like an angel's dream.

By the last notes of the song, we are at her bedroom door. We set our beers on the bed stand and fall into the pillows. She is a wonderful lover in ways only a mature woman can be and by the time we went back out to finish our beers, I knew I was deeply infatuated with her.

We sit at her kitchen table, sharing a beer, looking at each other across the table.

"That was fantastic. But this is all new to me, I'm taking a chance here, still I gotta ask. What's your name, beautiful? Mine is Matt."

She starts to laugh. "I suppose that is the kind of thing that would frighten you, I know not much else does. My name is Sherry. You can call me Sherry baby, or beautiful, or sweetie, or whatever else you want to call me as long as you keep calling me."

"Well Sherry baby, now that we have the heat burned off, how would you like to spend an hour or two enjoying ourselves?"

"Yes. I knew you would be a considerate lover. How would you like a nice big homemade breakfast with hot coffee?"

"I would love it," I said. "Because I will be cooking it in another seven hours, give or take a couple of hours, and you're welcome to stay here and wait for it. I'm free until tomorrow at two. We might need a little rest before then."

We headed back to the bedroom.

I left Sherry at eight the next morning. Lit a cigarillo, and strolled along, lost in happiness and thought. I circle into Frank's backyard and shout at him through the open kitchen window. He comes out to sit beside me. My cigar is still going.

"What's up?"

"Things are starting to shake loose. Something that we did is spooking somebody. Finally I'm certain that we're on the right track."

"Well tell me the good news, what's up?"

"Two guys in Chick's got a telephone call and then came over to start a fight with me. They had me targeted. I've been running it through my mind. I know I'm an irritating bastard, but I'm sure they were after me. So, who do we know that would send two men into Chick's to drive me out of town?"

"Maybe they were a little drunk and looking for a fight," said Frank.

"Not drunk, maybe looking for a fight, but the bartender warned me they had received a telephone call and both turned to look at me. These were two ordinary young men. They thought they could pick up a little extra money beating up an old guy. We need to find out who paid them. I'm telling you, Frank, we've poked a tender spot."

"That's good to know. Shows we're on the right track. We'll get ahold of that bartender tomorrow, see if he knows them."

"No need for that, I asked already. Bartender is a lady, by the way, and she didn't know them."

9
The Card Game

D'ANGELO IS SITTING across from me, we're finishing off the last of the coffee, phone rings. It's Sherry.

"Hey, Matt, I'm having a private game at my place tonight. Texas Hold 'em, one and two, no limit. Interested?"

"Certainly, what time is the game?"

"We'll meet about seven thirty, game starts at eight sharp. Yanks won, so I'll have plenty of cash for you."

"How about I come a little early, say around six. I'll bring some steaks and we can talk, maybe even put on some dance music?"

"Well," she says, "steaks sounds good. Why not come over at four so we'll have plenty of dance time?"

As a gambler, I have to keep an edge. Alert, aggressive, keen-eyed, all are very necessary to winning in poker. Assuming I wasn't playing with beginners, it can be difficult to pick up a tell. Without a good read on your opponents, it's like tossing your money into a pot and drawing cards to see who wins. An afternoon of delight with Lovely Lovely would be like polishing my edge with a hammer.

Still, I would have several hours to recover before the game. And there was the possibility of sex. Sex always wins in a man's thinking.

D'Angelo was in the living room trying to find out if the price is right. I sat at the table mulling over what little I knew. I can see an open end. This killer has been great at hiding his tracks, but the two men who attacked me last night were a mistake. It's possible that they were just out looking for a fight, but they would not have picked a fight with an old man over practically nothing if they were looking to have a real fight. They could have found a younger, more worthy opponent. Angry at me because I like the Yankees or because I was from out of town just seems too farfetched. They had to know who they were looking for.

Sherry had said she didn't know them, but that she had seen them before. So they had to live somewhere in the vicinity. The best way to find them would be to ask the other four men in the bar if they knew who they were. Sherry should know their names. Probably be better for me to leave Sherry out of this. She may begin to feel like she's being used.

Two options presented. Someone had told the two to look for me or I had been spotted going into the bar, and he had known the two men were already inside drinking. I had not noticed many cars that night, but there is always some traffic. Then again, just walking through town late at night makes you visible to anyone looking out a window. I could have been spotted from one of the other bars or even someone in the bowling alley.

She answered the door with a cold glass of wine which she handed to me.

"You're looking pretty good tonight, Matt."

I'm not so sure of that. I had on old blue jeans and a golfing tee. She, on the other hand, was spectacular. Her blouse was a light green silk piece and her skirt swept down to her ankles with a long slit up the side reaching to her hip. Sarah Vaughn was singing something sultry about Vermont. I took the glass of wine and she slid easily into my arms, feeling the way only a lovely graceful woman can. Murmuring small nothings to each other, we finished the wine and two more dances, before we began to feel a little sleepy and decided to take a short nap before eating. Sherry is certainly the type of woman that men search for all their lives. Her eyes have a depth that holds one's heart entranced.

We took a long slow shower together. I went out to put the steaks on her grill by six and poured myself a gin and tonic, small amounts of gin and large amounts of tonic. Smells and tastes like a much stronger drink. I dipped my finger in the gin and wiped some on my chin and shirt. There seemed no good reason not to appear more intoxicated than I was for the game.

This was Sherry's day off, but the phone rang frequently and she was rather busy writing down the bets coming in, and then relaying the info to her book.

She told me she took the bets, reported them up the chain, and kept half of the vig from the losers. Pretty low class. Illegal to be sure, but with little chance of being busted and it more than doubled what she made at the bar.

By seven thirty, the players began arriving. It seemed that everyone knew each other. This game, as it turned out, was a weekly ritual amongst the friends. I had been recruited to replace Dan Johnson, who was on duty tonight. Most of the players brought bottles of liquor or twelve packs of beer. The price of admission. I acted as bartender and mixed drinks for everyone. Mostly they drank bourbon and branch or beer. I was the only gin drinker. Greg was the only non-drinker, staying with Diet Coke. George, the local butcher, brought a platter of tiger meat and crackers. We all donated five dollars to him.

Sherry led us all downstairs to the circular poker table, very well lit with LED lights. They are so much easier on your eyes than the standard fluorescents. Nicely padded chairs on rollers, and plenty of room for drinks and snacks. Okay," says Sherry, "everyone knows the rules: one hundred dollar buy-in, one for small, two for large, no limit, Texas Hold'em. Here we go. She dealt each a card face up, Greg caught the ace of spades and was the dealer/button.

Judy, the small blind, threw in a buck, and Steve, the big blind, threw in two, while Sherry dealt. I had crap cards and mucked my hand. Judy bet five and no one called, winning the hand.

"Can't win them all if you don't win the first." A traditional stupid statement made after every first hand in Texas Hold'em. The deal made it around the table twice with me drawing nothing and mucking all hands except the big blind, and in those two hands, I drew nothing on the flop.

I excused myself from the table, "Time for a jolt of gin. Maybe that will improve my hands or at least will let me lose without caring." Everyone wanted a refill, so they held up the game while we refreshed. Once we were seated and Sherry was shuffling the cards, I held up my glass. "Here's to our missing man, Dan Johnson. He has an easy laugh, I'm sure he'll be back next week."

The gin might have helped, because in the next hand I caught a pair of sixes in the hole. Easily the best hand I'd see. I called the two dollars when my turn came. The flop came with a four, five, and six of spades. George raised another twenty-five. Steve called, and I called. The turn card was a king of spades, which I'm figuring gives someone a flush. George checked, Steve checked, and since I got what looks like the losing hand, I check. The river card is the king of hearts. George checked his bet, Steve bets twenty-five. He's the flush I figure, and raise my last forty bucks. George snap calls me. Damn, he's probably got a king and five in the hole. Steve hems and haws, looks at his cards, scratches his head, then calls. Steve flips over the ace of spades, I turn over my full house, and George turns over his pair of fours in the hole. Both jumped when they saw me turn my winning sixes.

They both rebought and the game went on, but at least I had gained a little credo and a much fatter stack. I had learned a few things about the poker players gathered tonight. Steve is willing to put in big money to chase straights and flushes, Judy will stay with little but an ace, and George puts a chip on his cards if he is going to keep them. If I look over and they are uncovered, a small bet will make him muck his cards.

Finally we took another break, refreshed our drinks, and attacked the tiger meat. I was eating and talking to everyone, when Steve touched my shoulder.

"That was a nice toast you made to Dan. Kind of surprised us. He is always grousing about you cause you are too close to Frank. Says you sway his judgement. That is always like Dan. He complains all the time: the weather, the shift he got, his car, it is always something."

"Must be unpleasant working with someone like that," I said.

"Yeah, it's something I thought you would want to know. All the people in town like him. Those of us that work with him are far less enthusiastic."

"Thanks, Steve. Actually I have no great feelings for the man, the only reason I made the toast was because I was taking his place at the table."

I grab George, by the arm, as he was walking by. "You were in the bar with me the other night, weren't you?"

"Yep. That was quite a show. You fried that guy's onions."

"Do you know who those two guys are?"

"I've seen them around. They're brothers, live on their family farm over near Avon. Never did hear a name for 'em."

"Thanks, I know I'll steer clear of them if I see them again."

Everyone was slowly heading back and sitting at the table. I took my seat. The game went on for another hour. I had found out what I wanted. With that information Frank should be able to find them. I was up just a little, should have let everything go with that, but I got a pair of eights in the hole. Anders raised ten, called by Judy, George, and Greg. This looked to be a significant hand. Let's see what they are up for. I called and raised twenty. Everyone called. The flop came down ace, queen, and ten of hearts. Yikes, three over cards, a possible straight, and a possible flush. I was in a bad place. When in doubt, be aggressive, make a continuation bet to keep everyone off balance. I raised twenty-five and all four called. The turn came as the eight of hearts. I have a set of eights, but there's got to be a flush out there. Maybe I can convince them that I have the king of hearts. I bet a hundred dollars. Judy and George both fold. Crap, I was hoping everyone would fold. When the bet got to Greg, he went all in and both Anders and I called. Since I was all in too, we turned the cards over. Anders had the king of hearts, Greg had the jack of hearts, Anders would win unless I paired something on the board. The queen of clubs flopped, giving me a full house. I raked in a ton of money. Damn, it felt good. The game broke up after that, no one wanted to rebuy. Since I was up, I was happy.

As the last of the group left, I swept Sherry into my arms and kissed her.

"You make a day wonderful just by being in it, beautiful."

"I feel the same about you, Matt. Can you stay the night?"

"Sorry, I would worry Frank and D'Angelo too much. Call you in the morning."

"Who is D'Angelo?"

"He's a young man living with me until he can get on his feet. You would really like him, got a great personality."

"When can I meet him?"

"I'll set up dinner this week. Best time to meet him, because what he does best in this world is eat."

10
Matt

AT ZERO LIGHT the next morning, D'Angelo knocks on my door. "Let's give it another try down there."

"Oh hell, yeah, gimme five minutes You looking for fish down there or visitors?"

"Fish, but she sure was pretty."

I drive to the park looking for any lights on in town, but there's nothing. Can't even score a cup of coffee. Twenty minutes later we are casting in the faint light given by the park's lamps. I doubt we'll catch much until the sun pops up a little.

"I wouldn't mind catching a few just in case she does show again," he says.

"I know what you're saying. She did seem grateful for the fish." I went back to working my Royal Coachman, I'm glad that D'Angelo has found something he really likes.

Soon a purple-pink light begins to be reflected on the water. Now I figure we'll have a better chance at catching something.

D'Angelo caught a skip jack and threw him back. "Want something just a little bigger."

"Yeah, those are fun to catch, but not much good as table fare."

I felt a cold chill at my back. I let my fly float and glanced behind us. There was a large man standing fifty feet behind us watching us silently, too dark to make out his face. He looked to weight over two hundred and fifty pounds. Dressed in baggy shorts, a large shapeless tee, and running shoes with a large NB imprinted on them. I couldn't imagine a man that large out running in the early morning.

I had a distinct feeling of danger and shifted my rod into my left hand. My right hand slipped into my pocket and I palmed the .38 I carry. D'Angelo laid his pole down and turning to the man, greeted him.

He had gotten close enough that I could see it was Deputy Johnson. "Don't get between us," I said quietly to D'Angelo, "Just in case."

Dan walked down and stood near us with a large smile on his face.

"'Hi guys, I was just jogging by and stopped to say hello. Heard you were are the game last night and had a lot good luck. Congrats."

"Good morning, Dan," I said. "Nice to see you again. Want to join us? I have an extra rod in the car you could use."

"No, thanks, never was much of a fisher. Well, better get back to my road work, see if I can lose some of this tire." He turned and jogged slowly off toward the entrance to the park.

"You seemed a little skittish there, Matt," said D'Angelo.

"I'm here investigating a murder, and I have no idea who committed it. Right now I'm feeling like a target, and I don't want to end up floating face down in this cold water."

It is all catch and release this morning. To D'Angelo and me that means we didn't hook anything spectacular enough to take the time to clean and cook. D'Angelo is very quiet as he works his line. I watch him for a few minutes. His skill for the few times we have been fishing is impressive. Maybe he has found something he likes as well as eating and looking at cute girls. When I mention the diner for breakfast, he packs his gear quickly. "Sounds good to me." I suspect he is a little tired of my oatmeal and scrambled eggs every morning. One great thing about him is that he never complains about food. He's turned out to be a good traveling companion.

We had not yet stopped at Tindale's main restaurant, The Breakfast Nook, but I could see a wistful look in D'Angelo's eyes every time we drove past. After the two fruitless hours spent by the river of fishing, hot coffee and warm food appealed to me too.

I had been here several years ago. I knew they served good breakfast food and great coffee, but the owner had not put any money into improving the aged, shabby exterior. The whole place still smelled of old grease and the ammonia cleaner they used to wipe down the cheap plastic that covered their booths and the Formica counter. The interior was bright with the hard glow of fluorescence.

I ordered us both a cup of coffee as we walked in. They had two waitresses now. One was Carol, she had been here when I was last in town. I didn't as yet know the name of the new girl. We slid into the empty booth. Carol brought the coffee over. "Nice to see you again, Matt. Heard you were back here in Excitementville."

"Nice to be back. Meet my friend, D'Angelo. D'Angelo, this good looking young lady is Carol."

"Too early to be blowing that smoke at me, Matt. Just tell me, what do you want to eat this morning?"

"Bring us both a Breakfast Mess, if it's still on the menu," I said.

"You got it," she said, walking away. "Mess them both," she shouted back to the kitchen.

"You're going to love this. It has layers of flavor and it just keeps tasting better."

"She didn't come to watch us fish today," he said.

"I noticed that. Fishing is always more fun with an audience. Maybe we ought to try out at the lake tomorrow. See if the tourists at Lewis and Clark Lake would like to come out to watch. Maybe we can even catch some fish out there."

"Whatever you think, but I like the place we're fishing at just fine."

"Well, let's stay there one more day. Maybe she'll show up tomorrow. She does look like someone who would be fun to talk to."

D'Angelo doesn't say anything. Looks at his coffee, quietly. I swear, I think he's blushing a little.

Once the food arrives, I hear nothing but silverware hitting plate. He invests little time with chewing. He could have done a backflip off the top of the stool into that Breakfast Mess and eaten the whole thing before he hit plastic.

"Lordy, Matt, you right again. It just kept getting better and better. I'm putting in my diary tonight that it was the best food ever."

"You keep a diary?" I am surprised.

"What you crazy? Diary is for ten year old girls."

The door is opened with the noisy bell jingling, I look up and see Pastor John walking in. He's beaming his big smile, face like an onion. There is something I just don't like about this guy.

D'Angelo says, "I'm heading back, if that's okay. I want to stretch my legs out a little, and get a look at this sprawling metropolis."

"Sure," I say. "See you at Frank's. I'm going to relax here and finish my coffee."

Pastor John shouts, "Coffee, Carol." Turns to me, "Mind if I sit for a minute?"

I motion with my hand that the seat is open and he slides in.

"It's another beautiful day here in God's country. How are you enjoying your stay?"

"Well, we're doing pretty good. Fish are hungry and it's nice visiting with Frank again."

"Too bad you can't hang around for another month or two. Up until it actually snows, the countryside just gets better every day. Yesterday my wife and I went out and picked an autumn display right out of the ditches on the side of the road."

There is something wired wrong with this turkey. I think of him like a dented can in a box of food, maybe it's okay, but it would be the last one you open. Seems to me, he was born twisted just a little.

"That does sound nice," I say. "But we'll be heading out of here in another week or two. Things to do, people to see. Besides, Frank will be going wild by that time to get rid of us."

"By the way, Matt, do you remember Al and Janet Cobb? I was with you when you met them at Margo and John's funeral."

I nod yes.

"I saw them earlier, and Al wants to talk to you about what he remembers on that Sunday when Slug got killed. Said he would be home most of the day, mentioned he'd be working on his yard.

"I'll probably spin out there and see what he wants. You take care, Pastor. See you soon," and I head out to the Explorer.

11
Al and Janet

JANET AND AL live three and a half miles north of Tindale, on a well maintained country road. I turn into their lane and am immediately impressed. The lane is wide and heavily covered with fresh gravel. Janet and Al have put time and money into making their house very nice. The right side of the lane is planted with fruit laden Bradford pear and apple trees. The lane is bordered on both sides by multi-colored daylilies. I know someone has spent a lot of time maintaining them. The lawn has been mowed close all the way to the house. Their home is a two story frame structure covered over by a metal roof. It's surrounded on two sides by thick tree growth. Strength to keep them safe during the heavy winter snows and trees to break the wind.

A huge still-painted red barn stands off to the right of the house next to a large Quonset hut. Sixty years ago, only the military was using these rounded steel buildings, but for the last forty years they were popping up on a lot of farms. Cheap to erect, roomy and strong, they are the new garage for machine storage for farms in the Midwest.

Inside the Quonset, at the rear of the building, sit Ralph and Buttrum, two men whom Al has hired to help him. Ralph has worked with Al for six years already, Buttrum is a friend of Al's. They were playing canasta and waiting. Al had told them the man who was coming was in his sixties, but still dangerous. If he was allowed to keep digging around and poking his nose into everything, he would find out their secrets and ruin their way of life. Buttrum had asked Ralph what the hell kind of secrets they could have, to which Ralph responded with he's probably going to bust up their Sunday night Bingo game. Well-muscled young men, they had no worries about beating the crap out of one old man. The five hundred they would share would pay their way out to Vegas for a short vacation. They want the man to show up soon, the smell of the Quonset hut housing all the older machinery is stinking of rats, gasoline, and old jugs of herbicide still sitting around.

I park in front of the hut, looking around for Al, whom I had thought would be out mowing his yard. The yard is trimmed nicely, but clearly it hadn't been mowed today. Still, with my tummy full on a beautiful day when I am coming to meet a friendly older couple, I'm not as alert as I should be to any danger. I leave my pistol in the car, under my front seat. The unexpected is what kills.

I step out of my car to a greeting by a large overly friendly Lab who has come bounding out of the garage. He's still half puppy and loves the smell of my shoes. He's jumping and racing wildly around me in greeting. A very nice dog. Considerate of Al and Janet to have chosen a black dog. Most black dogs are put down because of the difficulty in selling them or finding them a permanent home.

I walk the twenty yards to the front door, still looking for a door bell, when Al come outs. Janet is standing behind him, staying on the screened in porch, while Al steps out and stands on the top step of the entryway.

"Hi, Al," I say. "How are you doing this beautiful day?"

"I was doing much better before you came to town, City Man. I wanted to have you come out today, so we could tell you that you should have stayed where you belong."

The unfriendly response surprises me. "I don't understand, Al. What is it you want?" I suddenly don't like Al very much. The hair on my neck is standing straight out, warning me of danger.

"I have a message for you. One you won't like. I'm not sure how you nosey son-of-a-bitch got the idea you could come out here and mess with our lives. But enough is enough and my message to you is not going to be the spoken kind." He brings his right hand from behind his back, showing me that he is holding a construction hammer. The head of the hammer is slightly enlarged and the shaft is three to four inches longer than a normal hammer. It looks lethal in Al's gnarled old hand.

"Damn, Al, you think I'm going to let you get close enough to me to use that?"

"Not without help. That's why I asked them to be here." He looks behind me. I turn to see two large well-muscled men, looking to be in their late twenties to early thirties. They had come from the dark of the Quonset hut. The hut I had not bothered to check. They are still twenty yards behind me.

Al is starting to walk down the entry steps, maybe six feet from me.

"I suggest you stay with a verbal warning today. I really don't want to hurt anyone," I say. The heavy muscles have already closed to about fifteen yards, each has a stupid looking smile on his face. I suspect they think they look more threatening with a moronic smile. They've watched too much television.

"Hurt away old man," says the taller bulkier man.

"You know you don't want to do this," I say, talking fast just to keep them busy.

"Back off, walk away, and I will call no foul." I am turning so I can see all three men while backing off to my left away from them. They have closed in, so they are between me and the Explorer. Damn, I could use that pistol about now.

Al, on my left, swings the hammer at my back, with a wide sweeping blow. I push hard with my left leg trying to avoid the hammer, but the force causes my right knee to buckle. I go down on my right side close to the shorter of the two men. As I fall, I pull my fish filleting knife from the sheath on my left ankle and quickly switch it to my right hand. The knife's blade is razor sharp, but it has a very thin blade and I know it would be chancy to stab with. A piece of leather or a bone will snap the blade.

The short man grabs me by the back of my shirt. "Get up old man, you are going to get the beating you've needed for some time." I suspect he thought he was coming to a boxing match.

I lay the blade flat against his shin and as he pulls me up, I twist it and slice hard. I cut him deep and straight from the knee up to his groin before he even begins to feel the pain. As blood spurts, he releases me and screams. Both of his hands drop as he tries to stem the flow of blood from his leg. I slash rapidly at his arms and chest and am rewarded by the sight of more blood pouring forth.

Standing now, holding my blade in front of me, I back away from the two remaining men.

"You've lost one man already. If you hurry, you can save his life. I'm not a man to be merciful." My breath by this time is coming in ragged gulps. I am tiring fast. I still have the skills learned in the Special Forces, but I no longer have the strength or endurance.

Al and Ugly keep coming at me. Slowly, now that they know how much damage the blade can do, but relentlessly, they advance.

The injured man screams for them to help him. "Don't let me die here, Ralph. Ralph, you gotta help me." Big Ugly's name must be Ralph.

Ralph turns to look at the downed man. I whirl on my left leg and slice rapidly at Al. I miss him by at least a foot and he quickly swings the hammer again, but several seconds too late to hit anything. Hell, Al's reflexes are even slower than mine. I glance quickly at Janet who has left the porch and is walking to the wounded man. I refocus my attention on the younger man, a mistake, should have watched Al. He throws the hammer at me while I am looking at Ralph.

The hammer hits high on my left shoulder and the weight of it bounces it up into the side of my face. Had Al aimed better or thrown harder, I would probably have been killed. As it is, the blow throws me over on my right side, crashing hard against the gravel driveway. I lose my grip on my knife with the stunning blow. The young man rushes at me hard, and Al is coming for me as fast as he can. I know the man, coward that he is, will try to kick my head to end this fast, and sure enough, as if on cue, he plants his left foot and puts everything into his right leg aiming at my head. I roll away to my left side, and his foot just grazes the right side of my face. I rolled back quickly, jerk my hand under his foot, and lift it as fast as I can, a couple of feet higher than he wants it to go. He lands flat on the packed earth with a surprised grunt. Up on one knee now, I keep lifting until Al smashes into me from the left side. We fall hard on top of the legs of the downed man. I slam my elbow hard and with weight into his groin. I am rewarded by a grunt of pain. Shifting what weight I can toward Al, I drive a hard punch into the side of his head. He flops over on his side. I doubt he has ever felt a good punch and is surprised by the pain. Twisting rapidly, I drive my left fist into the young man's testicles. It's a flush power stroke at a fully open and unprotected target, guaranteed to toast his coconuts. I can hear him puking as I begin kicking at Al's head. I've gained enough ground to stand and I pick up the hammer. Al is busy scrabbling on the ground to get as far from me as he can. I begin swinging the construction hammer at his legs and feet.

I hear a pistol report. Looking up to where Janet is standing, I see her put a round into the head of the wounded man. Casually, she lifts her arm toward me and pulls the trigger again. The power of the blow throws me over backward. My last thought before blackness is, "Deadlier than the male."

Janet walked to Al and helped him up. "Christ, old man, seems like I can't let you handle anything. That man almost killed the three of you."

"Shit woman, didn't think that old fuck could be that tough." They are both looking at the man, cradling his crotch. He had rolled onto one side and was breathing easier. "Better get him an ice bag so he can drive. I'll bring the Explorer over." They loaded the bodies of Matt and the younger man nto the back of the Explorer. Al helped Ralph get into the driver's seat and gave him the ice bag to sit on. "Janet, you bitch, you didn't have to kill Buttrum."

"He was dying. Did you really want to spend 20 years in jail to help him die in a hospital?" I did him a favor and you a favor. Now listen to me and listen to me good. You fuck this up, we're all facing a death penalty. Drive straight north until you hit county road 46, it will be the first hard surfaced road. Take it straight east to 29. Take 29 south until you are just past Sioux City, then exit at Hubbard and pull into the small park that's off to your left. The Missouri there is hard and deep. Stop the car about ten feet from the river, leave the engine running. Put this cement block on the accelerator and let it run into the river. It will never be found. Do you understand?"

"Yes. How will I get back?"

"Al and I will be about fifteen minutes behind you. Now listen to me. If there are people there, wait until they leave or we get there before you do anything. You understand?"

"We could have treated Buttrum here."

"We'll talk about it when we get back. Now get going." They watched the car go down the lane, turn the right direction up the gravel road, and finally disappear from sight.

"I swear, Al, the help we get these days is so fucking useless." She took Al's hand to help him and they walked back to the house. "You want me to drive so you can shoot him, or do you want to drive so I can shoot? Can't let someone that dumb run around holding our future in his hands."

The world comes back to me in short starts. I can't remember how I have gotten here. I look at the dirty roof of the Explorer. I can feel the road, the car is moving. It is just such an improbable place for me to be. I try to sit up but my body refuses. It reminds me that I am injured. I roll to my right side and look at a dead man. No mistaking his death, blank eyes wide open and staring. White skin on his face framing black hair. Buttrum, I remember now. I killed him. No, I just injured him. That bullet hole in his head killed him. My knife caused his death by forcing Janet to kill him. It's a hopeless feeling knowing I have deprived him of a future. I'd been forced to take action against him, forced by his own hand. Another death writ large on my ledger. I lie back and close my eyes.

Why are we in the back of the Explorer together? I try to see who is driving. I must have passed out then.

I regain what little sense I have left in the back of the Explorer. How had I been so stupid? Strolled casually into an ambush whistling Dixie into the wind. I knew at least one person, probably three people, had been murdered in this small town and I had acted completely stupid. My left arm refuses to move without setting off kettle drums and fireworks in my head. With my right hand, I find the bullet hole on the right side of my chest. Damn, the pain is real. The hole is small, so the front is the entry point of the bullet. The exit wound in back must be much larger. I need to stop the bleeding and find something to drink. My thirst is ferocious. The bullet must have broken ribs, maybe my collarbone or scapula. I know the exit wound will be larger and is probably still bleeding. I have a thirst so fierce it is difficult to blink my eyes.

The dead man next to me is layered deep in dried blood. His shirt has a slash across the front. I grip it and pull the bottom half from the man. I am trying to be as quiet as I can, which is probably nonsense, as loud country music beating through to the back must be muffling most of the sound. I roll the piece of fabric into as tight a ball as I can manage with my good hand and teeth. The taste of his blood is smooth and pleasant in my mouth. Saliva begins seeping into my mouth, helping to reduce the overpowering thirst. I stick the wad of cloth under my upper left shoulder, and force my body up onto it with my legs. I want to pack it as deeply into the wound as possible. I must have lost consciousness again, because I remember jerking awake when the Explorer turns off the paved road onto a bumpy back road, throwing me around. The car slams to a stop. I stay motionless hoping whoever was driving would believe me to be dead. The engine is still idling, when the front door is flung open. I hear the passenger side door open. "What the hell," I think, "Can he be picking up someone else?" I curl my legs up thinking I would kick the driver in the face when he reaches in to pull me out.

Instead, I hear the engine begin to race. The car jerks forward hard. This fool is driving rapidly downhill. The car smashes into something hard, and I am thrown against the front seat with the dead man, laying with half his body across me. I push the body off me and raise myself up with my good arm to take a look.

"Shit," I think, "this stupid bastard has driven into the river."

12
The Killer

THE KILLER WAS pleased with the way his plans are moving forward. How easy it was to find fools to do your work. He had picked out Thurman easily. The man advertised his weakness to anyone willing to look. He was obvious to the killer who thoroughly knew the same fault.

He'd been lucky. His wife had picked the church and he had gone along for appearance. Part of the grand camouflage of life. He was projecting the image of an upstanding citizen in this small town. On Sundays he sat proudly with his little family in the congregation. This is how you demonstrate to the people that you do have a strong moral character. Here in the Bible belt, church membership was important. He sang the hymns loudly and acted reverently with his kids, well-scrubbed and neatly dressed, sitting next to him. His children also attended Sunday school every week. By his second year as a member of the church, the pastor had approached him to be on the church council.

He'd quickly noticed Pastor John's active eyes. Seldom did a young girl or woman walk past him that he didn't check out her butt. The Pastor's own daughter, Melanie, always stood close to him as if leaning on him for support.

Last summer, he'd casually approached John with a friendly smile on his face. "You know, I believe we are cut from the same bolt of cloth. We look at all the young ladies walking past us and think, I could put that to good use."

"No, No, that's not what I am thinking. I'm trying to guide them down a path to righteousness. It is a turbulent and difficult time for the young."

"Sure," I replied, "but if you ever want to kick back and relax, give me a call. I have an extensive library of excellent quality candid pictures I think you would enjoy." I strolled back and joined my family.

He was stronger than I thought. It was two nights before he called. He was like a hungry trout eating at the fat worm and looking with fear at the hook. I invited him over that evening. Poured him a shot of tequila and opened us both a beer.

"You do partake of spirits when you're off duty, don't you?"

"Occasionally. I stopped by tonight to thank you and your wife for all the help and support you've given the church."

"Oh certainly, Pastor John. You give so much of yourself to the congregation. My family appreciates your leadership. Hey listen, since you're here anyway, think you'd want to take a look at my collection of fine art?"

I can see the sweat beading on his forehead, and I know I am right. He's not here to talk about the church, he's here to look at naked pictures of little girls. He takes a little drink of tequila and chases it with a swallow of beer. I casually refill his glass. A little something to help him loosen up and show the side of himself he has tried to keep hidden all these years. The first look in the book sets the hook, hard and firm. He's caught now, I just have to make sure the line doesn't break. His hands are trembling as he turns the pages. He finishes two more glasses of tequila and is working on his second beer when he takes time to look up at me. I notice he's left the book open to a picture of a particularly fetching eight year old nude.

"I've never seen anything like this. Where did you get this book?"

"I've been around John. And as you know, anything is for sale if you know who's selling."

"Do you think you could find one for me?"

"I am sure I can. It would take some time though, and they are very spendy. They cost three to four hundred each, which is more money than I can spend right now with the family. So what I was thinking, was that you and I could make our own little book. Not one we would put up for sale, but one we could keep to remember our little girls while they are still pure. We could try to get Melanie and Javase together and see if they would cooperate with us. Who knows, maybe they would even pose if we asked them to."

At the mention of Javase's name he trembled a little. I knew absolutely what rang his little perverted bell. He sat quietly for a minute, then agreed that it would be a nice way to remember them when they get older.

"I have a quiet place, John. When do you think you and Melanie can get some time to come and spend with us?"

Fool that he is, he is willing to sell his future and the future of his family for one afternoon spent with Javase, Melanie, and a camera.

Unfortunately, I think my time here is running short. This new guy has Frank all fired up to investigate Slug's murder. They had Thatcher as good as convicted, why not leave good enough alone? At least they haven't decided to look more closely into Thatcher's death. Maybe the group is right. Just kill Matt and everything will return to normal. I know better, nothing continues to run smoothly forever. If Javase was as stupid as Melanie, maybe. Javase may be a hot blooded, enthusiastic, little wench, but she can also be a conniving bitch. She has been willing and enthusiastic this far, but she is not to be trusted for long. Her age is working against her. She's not happy with the way things are now, and getting a little long in the tooth. Al and John have mentioned a plan to eliminate Matt. It would be great if they can succeed.

He is driving his car now, going out to see Al and Janet. Pastor John called him and let him know that Matt had been sent out to the ambush. This Matt is trickier than they would understand. It's possible though that they have actually succeeded. Four against one old man, seems like good odds. I suspect that tricky old bastard is sharp enough to beat pretty long odds.

He has just washed his car. It looks good, feels good roaring down the road. His windows are open, the freshness of the air helps lift his spirits. It's time to leave. He knows it, but the ending of a time so sweet keeps him hoping maybe it will all work out for just a little longer. He turns into the lane. Parks in front of the Quonset. There are no vehicles in the yard. No one comes out when he blasts his horn. He walks through the Quonset and sees where Ralph and Buttrum sat playing cards while they waited. It was still filthy with cigarette butts laying everywhere. Lazy bastards could have cleaned up after themselves. He walks around the driveway. Too much blood he thinks. Careless to leave such evidence uncovered. This could not have gone well. Still, where are Al and Janet, and why have they not contacted him?

He unravels the outside water hose from the storage wheel and uses it to sluice down the patches of blood. The bloody water does not sink easily into the hard packed driveway but he stays with it until it looks clean. He pulls the hose back up by the house, returns to his car, and goes to town. He catches a quick bite at the Nook, the waiting is driving him crazy. He has to find out what has happened. Better to use the police computer to find out if a body has been found in the vicinity. He circles the office and sees only Rosa's car is parked out front. It is normal for him to come in and get some paperwork done at his desk. Once he logs on, he quickly finds that a body has been found, shot to death at a park in Hubbard, just off the interstate. The body has been identified as a local handyman. Al and Janet, he thinks, cleaning up the loose ends. Janet's the hard case, she would kill easily. He'd better go down and find out if there is more flotsam to be taken care of. Within minutes, he is back in the car heading south. The fresh air does nothing to raise his spirits now.

13
The Gambler

I CAN HEAR the subtle whisper of water entering through pin-holes and the sloshing of water in the foot wells, as the Explorer rocks and twists in the rapid current. Fear has me in its icy grip. The cool wetness of the water moves slowly up my back, helping me to regain my senses. I roll painfully to my stomach and drink deeply. This thirst, this terrible thirst, begins to relent. I rebel at the injustice of drowning in the back compartment of my own car. Unsure of how far out into the river the Explorer has drifted, I still feel a stupid sense of pride in how well it has remained water tight. If it had less buoyancy, I wouldn't have drifted so far. Close to shore is good, middle of the river will be bad. Now the water has risen enough to lift me off the floor mats. My dead companion washes back and forth with the rocking of the car as it settles on the bottom. He comes to rest with his body halfway over mine. A cold water dance seemingly designed to fulfill his mission to destroy me, even after he is long beyond caring.

With my right arm, I grab the handhold over the passenger door. Trying to ignore the immobilizing pain and kicking my feet desperately to keep my face above the water, I pull myself over on top of the dead hired man. I can see now that the Explorer is completely under water. The windows are shut which gives me a little more time, but also closes down an easy way out. I try the door handle I can reach, no chance of opening it. I can hear the door mechanism click, push against it with what strength I can muster, but I can't force it open. I push against the side of the car with my feet and pull hard at the headrest on the front seat with my right arm and am able to get most of my body over the front seat. The headrest blocks my legs and I need to twist to find the release knob. I lift it out and let it fall. I finally work my right leg over and by diving my head deep in the foot well, am able to drag my left leg over.

I raise my head, take three deep breaths, plunge down under the steering wheel, and thrust my right arm as far as I can under the driver's seat. When I purchased this car in Florida I had accepted the salesman's suggestion and purchased a break-out hammer, just in case. With Florida's many deep canals and ponds, buying it just made sense. With my lungs burning and my chest starting to spasm in pain, I force myself deeper, pushing off the dashboard with my legs. My hand brushes over the hammer, but I can wait no longer and I go up for air. Now sitting in the front seat with my legs floating, I try to quiet my heartbeat and recover a little energy. There is less than eight inches of air left trapped by the roof of the car. I try to kick the passenger side window out. New Balance running shoes with soft soles are useless for breaking auto windows.

Inhaling deeply, I turn and dive beneath the steering wheel. I need to get that hammer. I feel it, grasp it, and push myself back up to the seat. I swing as hard as I can, but the water is too high and impedes my swing. I can't generate enough force to shatter the window. I try another swing. Still nothing. The water is above the window line now and I rest for a minute. I need strength for one more try. Searching down to my right, I pull hard on the door handle and it clicks open. Damn, how dumb can I be? Once the water level is above the door, the water pressure evens out, and the door opens easily. I push the door open wide and slide from a watery grave into the current of the mighty Missouri with lungs already on fire.

"Ten seconds, Matt, you can hold it for ten seconds."

I twist trying to look up, but in the gathering night, can see nothing. I am kicking with my feet and pulling up with my arm. I struggle to subdue the spasms in my chest that are trying to force this worn-out body to breath. Lungs don't know shit about water, they just know they want to be used when the carbon dioxide levels inside the body rise. An insidious voice deep inside begins to whisper, let it go, end the pain. I feel a trickle of strength left in this badly treated body. I fight hard against the empty feeling of life ebbing.

Remembering my Navy training, I blow out all my air into the neck of my shirt. The water soaked material holds some of the air. Reaching high, my right hand breaks the surface. My face breaks through and I inhale quickly. Fresh air, the sweetest of air. My chest swells before I am forced down again by the current. I spread my legs and right arm, willing my body to float. The full chest of air should help. It works, my face breaks the surface again. I blow all my air into my tee-shirt one more time, and it begins to balloon upward, while I inhale fresh air. Much of the air in my shirt leaks out and is lost, but the precious amount that is trapped helps with buoyancy.

Three more breaths blown into my shirt give me confidence in my ability to stay above water. My shirt looks like a Mae West. I need to get rid of my shoes, the anchors on my feet, and push hard, one foot against the other, until I dislodge them. I take another deep drink of water. It's a marvelous elixir and my deep thirst fires down just a little. I am actually beginning to think I might live through this. And the question blasts unbidden through my mind, "Now what the fuck am I going to do?" The water is stealing my warmth. I have to get to shore. Which way is shore? I hear Sergeant Pate laugh, 'Either way, Dummy, that is not with the current or against the current. Same as all rivers everywhere.'

I am smashed into hard by a downed tree limb. The sudden unexpected blow throws me over to my right side. I lose all the air in my shirt, and am just alert enough to get my right hand up to grasp a small branch and hold on hard. Slowly, I work my hand down the branch from thin to fat. Turns out to be a large limb, luckily only the outer branches hit me. Bracing myself for the effort, I swing my left leg up and over the branch. I keep scooching myself along trying to get square enough to remain seated on the branch. I find rough tree bark and tender water soaked genitalia are not good friends. My last thought I before I passed out was, "Maybe I'll live, hope I'm still a male."

An irritatingly bright light is being shined directly into my eyes forcing me to awaken. I fight back not wanting to open them. I force them open, knowing I must blink a few times, then they close to avoid the electronic brilliance.

"Mr. Smith, Mr. Smith, are you awake?"

"Yeah, yeah, I'm awake, just don't want to talk." I'm still foggy and grouchy under the effects of heavy sedation.

In the recovery room, I can hear the movement of others waking and talking quietly to the nurses. My arms and legs feel leaden. I'm very cold, body shivering, and my brain feels like it's coming out of a three day tequila binge.

"Mr. Smith, can you open your eyes?"

When I look at her, I see the nurse is in her early thirties, short brown hair mostly tucked under a paper cap, intense green eyes, very thin, almost anorexic appearing. She is wearing light blue scrubs. Her scrub's blouse is unbroken, hanging straight down. I speculate that she has not had breast enhancement surgery.

"How did I get here?"

"A couple of fishermen saw you on a tree limb and called 911. I heard that they picked you out of the river with a helicopter."

"Okay, okay," I mumble, "I'm awake, can you get this torture slab into a sitting position for me, please?"

"No. It's too early for that. How do you feel?"

"Feeling great, sweetheart. Just give me a few minutes to rest here."

I'll be back soon," she says. "Just rest. Everything went okay." Then she leaves me. Hustling off to help someone else.

God, I hate hospitals, I hate doctors, but mostly I hate nurses. They are the pain inflictors in mankind's quest for healthy bodies. If you have a place that hurts, they want to poke it. If you have a place that should be private, they want to look up it. My mind is the only truly diseased part of me anyway. It is a totally male mind with all the strangeness that necessitates. Thanks to all divine powers that have left me a relatively clean, dirty old man, who enjoys watching the cheerleaders during Monday Night Football, as much as watching the behemoths smash into each other. I am drifting on the residual effects of anesthesia. I have never responded well to anesthesia and my mind is now replaying a vision of an extremely cute Dolphin cheerleader doing a back flip when I turn my head and look through the window of the recovery room. My heart jumps to one hundred and fifty beats a minute at least. It's Deputy Johnson from Tindale. I'm sure one of the deputies is the killer, I know he shouldn't be here. How could he possibly have found me? Still, there he is. If that really is him, I doubt he is here to rescue me. Now what? How can I possibly get out of here before he finds me? I have no weapon to defend myself here.

He's talking to someone. Not looking at me. Maybe he doesn't know I'm here. No that's just silly. He's here for me. I'm vulnerable. Since I can't move, I lay still. Then I see who he is talking to. It's Chocolate Chips, my nurse. They turn to look in the recovery room and she points at me; obviously explaining something to him.

Well, not much I can do but accept the inevitable. At age sixty-two, I have had a good run. Made it through a war, kissed at least three beautiful women, and have three wonderful children. None of whom will have anything do with me. Still they are or were all a beautiful part of the wonder of my life. I could close my eyes and relax. My mind accepts that sometime in the next twenty-four hours, I will probably be dead. Well, what the hell, after age sixty-five I figured I was out walking on the ice anyway. I vow that if I live and after I shake this chemical imprisonment, I am going to reconnect with those I loved in my life. It can't be too late already, maybe some of them will still talk to me.

As the darkness descends on me again, I think, "Do not go wild. Stay in control. Ignore the nightmares." It's too late, I can feel the heaviness of the humidity close in hard. Breathing is difficult and accentuates the heavy thrusts of air from the rotors. Lights are everywhere. Flashing about, flares are lit, the .88's put some high in the air and the landing zone force had placed some on the ground. Helicopter lights are burning swirling holes into the night. It's a chaos created by mad minds and war lovers. I am carrying the back of a stretcher. I know I need to hurry. Running, lifting, do not look around in the dark, don't think, most of all don't think. It's a friend of mine on this stretcher. Epstein, one of my corpsmen, has taken a round that gave him a sucking chest wound. As I push him onto the Huey and safety, I feel the pressure and breeze from a round pass inches from my neck. The round lifts Epstein off the litter and leaves him crumpled on the far side of the Huey.

"Take off," I scream to the Huey crew, "You're loaded." I run for safety, as if there really is any, in the maelstrom of the heat, lights, and death. The heavy coppery smell of Epstein's blood which had sprayed out, covers me. I'm sure my company must be near here. I know I will be safe if I can find them. Nothing can happen now. Then the lights slowly click off, one by one, and I sink deep into black.

I'm swimming hard. Cold thick heavy water pulls at me, my lungs burn with overused air, but my hand breaks the surface, and I come out with my head sucking air.

I'm in a hospital bed. It's all been a bad anesthesia driven night-mare. I'm safe. I breathe. Lights are on. People are close by. I am safe. I hear my nurse come near. She makes sure I am well covered with a blanket. Several men in blue scrubs and face masks gather around me, click something on the bottom of my gurney. They move me out of the recovery room down a long hall, up in the elevator, then down another long hall to a semi-private room. There is a man already in the room. He's curtained off. They move me from the gurney to the bed. She shows me how to raise and lower the bed, turn on the television set which sits high on the opposite wall, and of course, control the morphine pump. By now, I am coming out of the haze. I can pretty well comprehend what she is telling me. My brain is starting to work properly and I have calmed down, trying to forget the bad dreams. There is no war, there is no Dan Johnson, all hallucinations.

As she starts to leave, my nurse turns to me and says, "The doctor will be in to see you in a few minutes. Use as much morphine as you need tonight. The machine will not let you take too much. Oh, I almost forgot, your brother stopped me in the hall to ask how you are doing. He said he would stop by tomorrow. He is very concerned about you. Seemed like a nice man."

I guess I'm not as safe as I thought. I have no brother. "Damn, Matt," I think, " You really did see Johnson through that window. What do you do now?"

" Nurse, Nurse, is my billfold in here?" I need to keep people around to be safe.

She turns back into the room and points to the cabinet next to my bed. "It's right in there, in the top drawer. It's locked, but here is the key. Your clothes are in the closet."

"Would you take some money out and buy me a Coke? I really need something sweet and wet."

"I can't do that, but I'll order a soft drink to be delivered with your evening meal. There is a container of ice water there on your stand. If you need anything more, just push that button." She heads out of the room. Her many duties call.

I've just had surgery to repair a bullet wound on my left shoulder. I am lying quietly trying to regain my strength and marshal my thoughts when the doctor comes in.

"Well, Mr. Smith, your surgery went very well. The bullet wound is closed and we've started you on antibiotics. Soaking your wound with a dirty rag and Missouri river water is never recommended. I could see no real problem but we will know better in a few days. I think we may stay with the intravenous antibiotic therapy, but we can talk about that later. Just rest tonight and we'll talk again tomorrow."

As soon as he leaves, I begin to weigh my options. If I call law enforcement, they will brush me and my fears off. I'm just another old person who has been under anesthesia and now is afraid of the dark. They will never believe me. I don't really have or know anyone close enough to come and sit with me or bring a weapon for me. Easily, to my way of thinking, the safest course is to leave the hospital. I might just as well get at it. I struggle to sit up on the bed. A thousand stars explode behind my eyes as I pull on the metal bed frame. Twice I am unable to withstand the pain and fall back. Finally, I sit up. It takes a few moments to get my balance right, with my legs over the side of the bed, and head up high. The fog has pretty well cleared from the operating system of entity, Matt. The wound site on my chest is the most painful, but my whole body hurts from the fight and the escape into the river. If I don't use my left arm, it doesn't hurt, but to reach and grab with it is excruciating. I find myself leaning to the right to take the weight off my left hip. Whatever escape plan I come up with from here is going to be a beauty. If I try to run, my wound may reopen and I could bleed to death. If it becomes infected that could also kill me but more painfully and over a greater span of time. If I just rest and go to sleep, Deputy Johnson will be here to turn my lights out. Fuck it, walk on, better to die trying on my feet. Christ, no one ever said life was going to be easy. Pushing with my right arm, and grimacing with pain, I manage to stand. The weight is all on my right leg. Waves of nausea and pain sweep over me. I stand still as a deep aching muscle spasm grips me, then turn and retch the small amount left in my stomach onto my bed. Pull the covers over it to hide it from view, and let my body adjust to the new situation. Take off the nose junk which is wrapped about my head, then pull out the IVs, and push the bottle holder back so I can walk without tripping over it.

I push the curtains back and try my first move over to stand next to the man in the bed next to mine. He is a gray-haired, pasty-skinned man, breathing loudly. I believe him to be in a coma. I start removing the sensors attached to me and place them on him. I know that if I just remove them, an alarm will sound. The last sensor, the one on my forefinger is removed and placed on the sleeping man's finger.

I move as fast as I can, which by normal standards would be considered granny gear in power setting. Pants put on first, then shoes just slipped on, can't bend over to put on socks, finish up with shirt, billfold, watch, and glasses. I try one step, pushing my left leg forward six or eight inches. Then pull my right leg back up even. That wasn't so fucking bad. I have spasms firing off from my toes up to my ears. I can't remember my ears ever cramping before. I stand quietly and absorb the pain. I can do this. Go now, take another step. I grab the curtain to maintain my balance. Let go and take another step. Two more and I am at the wall. The muscle pain is starting to recede from use. I follow the wall to the bathroom, enter one side, slide around the toilet, open the opposite door, and exit into the next room.

There are two older ladies who immediately stop watching television and start watching me.

"Oops," I say, "I was visiting Otis and got turned around in that bathroom.

Do you mind if I use your door to leave?" I ask on the move since I am already walking toward the door. I'm going so slow that if I lose momentum, I will be at a a total stop. Four short steps, open the door. Two steps, shut the door. Just like that, I am free. Out in the hallway by myself, I hold on to the door, now to regain my bearings. No screaming as yet from the ladies' room, the great hospital escape is well under way.

Can't walk past the desk or the nurses will see me, so I follow the signs to the exit. Well aware that once I start down, the doors will all be locked until the first floor, I intrepidly head down. This will be a battle as my room is 511. I take the steps slowly: left foot down, then right foot down to the same step. Down I go to the first landing. A few deep breaths, "I can do this." Five steps down from me, on the landing for the fourth floor, I see a man smoking a cigarette. He has the door blocked open.

"Oh my friend, I have been looking for you. Would you sell me a cigarette for a buck? They took them before my surgery and I'm dying for a puff."

He knows he would be fired if caught out here and would usually be spooky as hell, but he can readily believe another smoker would come out looking and he accepts me.

"You know I'm risking my job for this, I think I should get at least two from you."

"And a bargain at the price," I smile. I dig out my billfold, hand him the two bucks and accept a light from him. Stand quietly talking for a few minutes, to allay any suspicions, toss the butt into his soda can, and go into the hallway on the fourth floor. To the right, about thirty yards down the partially lit passageway, I see the elevator sign. Oh joy, oh joy. Life is much better with elevators.

I slowly stick my head out of the elevator doors. Nobody moving in the hallway. I see the red arrows leading off to my left. The legend sign on the wall says red leads to the Emergency Room. There is always an entry-exit at the emergency room and it is always open. I follow the red floor markings. Twenty minutes and forty turns later, I see the lights to the Emergency Room off to my left but I do not look into it as I walk slowly past. No one notices a person walking slowly past unless they turn to look at you. I walk out into the cool darkness and stand in the shadows by the covered entrance to the ER.

"What do I do now?" My medical problems and weak physical condition are obviously a major difficulty. I need a place to stay that will be safe and warm while I recover. Before I can do that, I need to find out where in the hell I am.

As I am standing there, thinking about my next move, a gray sedan pulls up, parks before the door, and leaves the engine running. An older man gets out of the passenger side and starts to walk, stiff-legged, bent forward at the waist, toward the entrance. He stops, stands on his toes, and vomits long onto the road. He looks terrible. I can see the greenish gray of his face under the harsh neon of the entryway. He stumbles to the wall, leans on it, and again his stomach empties.

"Wait, George," an older woman shouts, as she leaves the driver's side of the car and runs over to support him. She wraps one of his arms around her neck, leans in toward him so she is carrying most of his weight, and leads him into the Emergency Room, while I head for her car.

I manage to force myself behind the wheel and speed off into the dark. I have an attack of guilt stealing their car while he is obviously having a heart attack, but they will both be in there for better than an hour and perhaps I can be well away from here by then. In three blocks, I see Highway 29 and turn north, moving that rambling gray puppy up the streets to safety. In Sioux City, I take the first motel I see on the right hand side of the road. Rent a room, then leave the car, wiped down as best I can to remove my fingerprints, parked next to a phone booth with the keys still in it. It would be a great time for the neighborhood car thief to come by.

I check into the motel using a credit card without thinking of remaining hidden. They give me the room next to the office. It has all of the ambiance of the hospital room I have just left. Still it looks and smells clean. The sheets, when I pull the cover down, have that crisp, new feeling. Bland mass-produced ocean landscapes hang on the wall. I will just avoid looking at them, they could only make me feel sicker. I drink two large glasses of water, sit very gingerly on the bed, pick up the phone, and call Frank. I have to warn him about Johnson.

He's groggy, probably been asleep. "Yeah?"

"Frank, Matt here. I'm in Sioux City, just got out of the hospital. They tried to kill me yesterday. Dan Johnson was in the hospital. Be very suspicious of him. I'm still foggy from the anesthesia, will call and tell you everything in the morning."

I lean back slightly, and try to fall asleep as I aim my head toward a pillow.

Sleep doesn't come easily. I lie quietly in the bed. Pain radiates its warning to me. Something is totally wrong with the picture Tindale has given me.

I understand that Al, Janet, and the two thugs are involved. Why are they part of this? I believe Pastor John is also part of the conspiracy. He has to be in on whatever secret Al and Janet are trying so hard to keep. At least one deputy is involved, could more be involved? Is Frank a part of the conspiracy? Tindale appears to me as in a fog, with evidence strewn around, yet no lines to connect one piece of evidence to another. No faces are clear enough to identify. A hidden death is lurking in plain sight. An evil man that everyone trusts.

I slip into darkness finally, but this will not be a restful sleep. The lights overhead are swirling in a white fog of exploding shells. I am once again carrying the back of a litter, running toward a helicopter. I struggle to run fast in the dark weed covered ground. Terrified of the explosions and the rounds zipping past, I somehow know it's my friend on the stretcher. It's my friend Sluggo. He is shouting something at me but in the roar of the Huey, I can't hear him. As we push onboard, a round hits him and he is lifted and thrown to the far side of the chopper. As he goes, he extends his hand and tosses pictures at me. I grab but they are whirling away with the wind. I see several pictures in the dark, but am unable to recognize the faces. Dark figures in awkward poses. I go into a deeper sleep and the maelstrom fades. The pictures now are swirling in the updraft of my mind.

Sometime during the night, I turn over and pull the sheets and bedspread over me and realize I recognize her. It's Javase. Sluggo was showing me pictures of Javase. My body hurts when I turn over, but the residuals of the anesthesia and extreme tiredness let me sleep soundly through to the morning.

I walk across the parking lot in the morning to a mom and pop's breakfast place with a front patio. I stop at the gas station next door on the way and buy a package of cigarillos and a tooth brush. Damn, that first cigar always tastes so good. Seated at one of the patio tables, I order half a plate of biscuits and gravy, with a side of two eggs. The gravy is tasteless and the eggs are cold, but I sit quietly, savoring the beauty and flavor of life after a long night, when I thought mine was ended. The coffee is black and hot, my smoke is fresh. The gray car is gone. I feel safe for the moment.

Back in my room, I use the yellow pages to pick out a dentist. The third one I call will have time for a painful tooth I told him I chipped. Two hours is the soonest he can see me.

"I have an implanted artificial knee," I tell him, "Can you call in an order for an antibiotic for me to a local pharmacy?"

He takes all my information and tells me the address of the pharmacy. "You be sure to take the meds, right away. Come in a little early and I will try to work you in," he tells me. I take a cab to the pharmacy, then back to the motel. I relax on my bed. I need to rethink my friends and enemies here in South Dakota. Who do I dare call for a ride back? While I trust Frank and D'Angelo, the mole in the department seems able to find anything. I decide that I will just hitchhike back the seventy miles. If no one knows I'm coming, no one will be waiting for me.

I rest for the day. At twilight I begin the journey back. Two hours without a ride has left me with a bone-deep weariness. My body aches and complains bitterly as I stand in the dark. It is full night now and I am determined to make the next town, at least. I refuse to walk back to the motel. Two short rides, a gray old bucket of bones dressed in a colorful plastic shirt, who kept complaining about being an old man in an old car, takes me only five miles. Then in the mist, before the steady rain begins, a short guy in jeans and a western shirt picks me up in a loaded pickup and takes me to the turnoff at the interstate.

The dreariness of an all-night gas station is what light can be found. Rain keeps people from stopping and I stand waiting in the wet misery with my thumb out.

At last, a school bus stops. The doors swing open and the driver asks how far I am going.

"Next town would be great, have to get out of this abominable rain. "

"Jump in, buddy. I'm delivering this beast to Pierre. We'll see town long before then."

There are two drivers, one about forty and one in his twenties. The seats are hard but wide. The bus drives slowly, holding to a fifty mile an hour break-in. The two men, father and son, had taken on this job during their vacations, believing that a week-long delivery trip in a vehicle would be an interesting way to get to know each other better. Now three days later they have spent more than adequate time together. They want someone to talk to. I begin telling them a long rambling tale of being shot in the back in Key Largo, spending time in the hospital, and now needing to return to my daughter's house in Tindale, South Dakota, for a recuperation visit. As I talk I sink deeper into the seat.

"We're going right by Tindale, we'll drop you off at your sister's house."

The darkness rushing past me, barely visible in the rain, seems like visions of my life as we ride. Nothing can really be seen except the large wind breaks surrounding the occasional farm; just as my life looking back has long black times broken by larger black periods. This trip, like my memories, is such a meaningless part of life. The passing of each mile seems to emphasize my own inability to recognize the importance of each passing landmark. My travels seemed to lead me somewhere that I would soon leave, to move futilely forward to a new place, where nothing of importance or depth waits for me.

I have always hated violence. Too many people, too many family members, had lost years due to their service in World War 2. As a kid, I remember the haggard drawn looks on the faces of my father and uncles when they returned from the war. These men were and still are my heroes. They knew everyone and everything. They had time to spend talking to a skinny kid in dirty clothes. By the time I was a teenager, most had recovered; they had families, children of their own, and I rarely saw them. We were scattered across southern Minnesota, so the holidays were the only times we gathered. Now they seemed as normal as everyone else. Two had died, one by his own hand, and one was killed in a bar fight. I went to a movie set in Africa when I was six and was fascinated by the natives who carried and threw spears. I can no longer remember the movies name, but it starred the incredibly beautiful Ava Gardner. I was mesmerized. For years, I ran around with my six foot spear. It was only a long metal rod, but to me it was a romantic weapon. I remember my youngest uncle leaving a family reunion one Sunday and walking three blocks with me to watch me throw my make-believe spear at tin cans I had lined up. I was so proud when he acknowledged my ability with it. It's funny how the things of our childhood affect our whole lives.   With all my spear throwing, I developed a really strong right arm and a grip that could be overpowering. By the time I was a freshman in high school, I could throw a football further than the starting quarter-back. At a new school attended after my family moved, the reigning bad guy accosted me, threw two or three roundhouse punches, then I struck him once in the chest, breaking two of his ribs with the first punch. Not too surprising that no one else even tried.

I joined the service right after I graduated. In my mind, that's what men did. 'God and Country' was the mantra of my family. That I excelled in the military surprises me because I still hate violence.

The bus brakes and the opening door wakes me from my memories. I talk to them a minute and exchange names and addresses. I am certain we will never talk again, but some people just hate to say goodbye. I walk up to Frank's door and ring the bell. D'Angelo opens it and hugs me lightly.

"Damned if I wasn't starting to get a little worried about you."

"Nice to see you again too, D'Angelo. Sorry I was away so long."

We have dogs jumping all over us. It's nice to have been missed. Bogie doesn't settle down until I sit on the couch and he can crawl into my lap. Funny how much love can rest with a furry little tail-wagger. Frank finally shows up, wrapped in a robe.

"You really had us worried, Matt. Great to see you back."

"I've got a bunch to tell you, Frank. Afraid our case has taken on a whole new depth in a way I never saw coming."

D'Angelo leashed up the puppies for a quick walk. Frank sat down in an easy chair across from me.

"Want to run it past me tonight or wait until tomorrow?"

"Let's hit the high points now, we can sort it all out tomorrow. First, we got at least three people involved that I had not seen at all. Pastor John is in this somewhere. Al and Janet are deep into it. They tried to have me killed and ended up shooting me. Two more men were in it, one of them is under water in my Explorer. I don't know what happened to the other. My strongest belief now is that Dan Johnson is the head of the whole conspiracy, but I have no proof."

"Jesus. That is going to tear this community apart. What in the hell is going on that I wouldn't have a clue about it?"

"The answer all lies in Sluggo's death. I don't know why, or even how he found out, but I believe, knowing what you told me, that this all has to do with a sex ring of child abuse. He came to me in a dream, showing me a picture of Javase. I know it wasn't real, but it put all the pegs in a hole. Anyway, that's what I've found out and surmised. I have to go to bed now. My shoulder is killing me. I need a doctor tomorrow. Maybe you have some dressing here to bandage me up. At least I've given you a ton to chew on tomorrow. Nothing is happening until morning because no one knows I'm here. Still, let's keep the guns handy. We know these people are desperate. I'm going to file an insurance form on my Explorer tomorrow. Hopefully they have pulled it out of the river."

A shower, fresh bandages, and I fall into a fitful sleep. Too many weights on me, I need to talk to D'Angelo. I'm the one who put the saddle on, time to start carrying the weight.

After breakfast, when Frank had gone to his office, I pour another cup of hot coffee and call him in. He takes the chair across from me.

"D'Angelo, I want to apologize for getting you into this mess. I never saw this coming, now I'm afraid I've gotten you into it too."

"Matt, I'm getting three hots and I got a couch to sleep on. Best shape I been in years. Just super glad to see you back and kicking."

"I think you and me have to make a few plans. After all this crap has happened, mostly what I worried about was leaving you stranded with nowhere to go. So I been working on how to give you a hand if I bite the big one." I take a drink of coffee, stand up, and say, "Come on out back, I need a cigar to talk about all this with you."

I go out the back door, sit on the wooden steps, pull out a smoke, light it, and look at him.   "You okay after the last three days?"

"No problems. You scared the hell out of me, not coming back, but I always had faith that you'd be back. You would never just leave Bogie and Thunder."

"It was close this last time. I never saw it coming. Found out I got enemies I didn't know I had. So now, I want to get you papered up, so you can drive and work. That we have to do right away. We'll go down and talk to Rosa later. I also want to order those General Educational Development books, so you can get a diploma. With a driver's license, Social Security card, and a diploma, you'll be able to get by no matter what."

"I was hoping you could help me get the GED. I've heard of it, but don't know the mechanics of it. Don't want you worrying about me. I'll be fine."

"I know you'll get by, but I want you to succeed. I got an invest-ment in you. You're important to me. You down with my plan so far?"

"Absolutely."

"Anything you want to add?"

"I been thinking too. I got to get something going to earn some money. I need more clothes, and I want to get a bike. I suppose it seems dumb to you, but a bike would let me move around the town so much easier. It wouldn't seem like I was locked in. So if you or Frank hears about work I can do, let me know, okay?"

"I don't know of any work, but I will ask Frank. In the meantime, what I can do is make you a loan. I will loan you $1000. You have to pay it back to me when you reach 21. Until then, we won't talk about. You up for making a loan?"

"Fuck, that's a lot of money, Matt. Sure you can handle that?"

I take out my billfold and give him ten hundred dollar bills. "I can handle that much. Remember, it's a loan. If you run short, please let me know. I think that should hold you until you get your Social Security card."

"I been on the computer since you took off. I found my school records at Blue Island Elementary, and my baptismal certificate at Christ Church. Think that will be enough papers?"

"That's great, let's send for them."

"It's thirty bucks. How about if I set up PayPal, then we can put it on your credit card, and I'll give you the money."

"I'm good with that. Let's get started."

Ten minutes later, they were paid for and on the way.

"I think you ought to get over to the sheriff's office and pick up a book for your driver's license. Find out when they are scheduled. We'll be ready to go when I get a car."

He grabs his cap and is out the door. I swear, he has a smile on his face.

14
The Killer

THE BEST LAID plans bullshit always rears its ugly head. The circle he had woven together with such care was never meant to last. Old people die off, his bait is growing older. He'd had a good three year run, now it was time to look for better pastures. He had hoped Al and Janet could pull it off, but instead, they had shown everyone their cards before the last bet was made. Now they were just loose ends that had to be cut free, and fast. He was unsure how that old bastard evaded him at the hospital, but he knew way too much. He picked out a dozen doughnuts at the bakery and drove out to see Al and Janet at 6:30 a.m.

He walked to the kitchen door in the light rain that was falling, knocked at the door, and was let in by Janet.

"Al is out in the shed working on something. That old fool probably doesn't even know it's raining out." She went to the kitchen window, opened it, and gave him a shout. Looking in the bag, she gave a small squeal of delight.

"Fresh doughnuts. You want coffee?"

"Sounds perfect for the pastries."

She had three cups poured and the doughnuts set out on a plate by the time Al came in to wash his hands and pull up a chair.

"I wanted to thank you both for taking care of that big city fuck. Life will go on much better without him."

"I shot him center beam with the .38, then we dumped him in the Missouri in his car. We'll never hear from him again," said Janet.

The older couple were each munching with a doughnut in one hand and coffee in the other.

"I'm really here for business today. Pastor John came to me with some good suggestions, and since you two are an integral part of our group, I wanted to run them past you. He thinks we should buy a place, like an abandoned farm, where we could fix up a nice meeting place. Everything would be less suspicious that way, and we could install hidden video cameras. The kids act naturally if they don't see the cameras.

We also talked about publishing a book. We have beautiful models, there will be a lot of pictures taken, and the book sales will probably pay for everything. It will be a little touchy finding the right publisher, but I have some ideas in that area. The other thing is, we can keep the pictures we want, so we will have memories of the good times. What do you think?"

"I think it's a good idea," said Al. "A remote quiet place for new inductees is a must. Those boys made a lot of noise the first time."

"How much money are you talking?" asked Janet.

"$1000 each, for seed money. That should get a down payment, couple of beds, a few chairs, and of course, the cameras. Once we start making money, we'll keep improving the place."

"When do you want the money?"

"Today, if possible. That way, John can get started on the place, and I can pick up the video equipment when I go to Sioux Falls."

"Make it a thousand for both of us and we're in. If you want two thousand, we'll have to make a bank run."

"Just a thousand for both of you is plenty. You're such good friends, I was going to put your share in myself if you needed it."

"Janet can get it. Just wait a minute."

He waited quietly until he heard a loud click in the bedroom.

"I wish this could come out differently," said the killer as he drew his pistol and shot Al in the face. Al's chair went over backward. Al lay motionless. Moving quickly now, the killer ran to the doorway of the bedroom. Janet fired the pistol she was holding. The bullet buried deep into the door frame next to him. He shot Janet where she knelt in front of the open safe. She slumped forward and did not move. He stepped next to her and shot her twice more, then shoved her body out of the way with his foot.

"Don't have two thousand, my ass," he said. He went back to the kitchen, got the paper bag he had brought the doughnuts in and filled it with the money and jewelry from the safe. On the way out, he picked up his coffee cup and pushed it into the bag with the money and Janet's pistol.

Hells bells, he thought on the way back to town. Maybe my luck is starting to run better.

15
Javase

IT'S LATE MORNING, there is a gentle rain falling on a chilly autumn day. Javase needs the cold and rain. She has waited for just such a day. She can stand her life no longer and has developed a plan to escape. She calls the bank.

"Can I speak to Mr. Selvitz, please?"

"Please hold, he's on another line."

"I'll wait," she replies, expecting that he would probably be busy.

A long two minutes later, his gruff voice comes on the line. "Yes, what can I help you with?"

"Mr. Selvitz, it's Javase, LeeAnn's friend. I just had a blow-out fight with my mother. I need help and I couldn't think of anyone else to call."

"Well Javase, I think you should go back home and apologize to your mother. I'm sure she loves you and is trying to do her best for you."

"So you won't help me then? I always thought you were so kind."

"I don't see anything I can do."

"I'm freezing in this rain. I'm hungry and broke. I just want to get something to eat and get warm for a little. Is that asking too much?" Her voice was weak and plaintive.

"No, Javase, that's not asking too much. Where are you? I can take you to get something to eat and let you warm up in the car."

Javase was wearing a short, black and white, pleated skirt, with a slightly tight white blouse as she slid into the seat next to him. Her skirt rode up high on her legs giving George a quick flash of a perfect inner thigh as she reached back for the seat belt buckle. She lay back against the Cadillac's soft seat, and relaxed. She did not notice how high up in her lap her skirt had ridden and did not adjust it further down. She could feel his eyes prying at her skirt before she turned to look at him.

Selvitz, now in his late forties, could not believe the vision of beauty and sexuality sitting next to him. He wondered how he could innocently extend this time. Maybe God would let him trade in Penny Ann for Javase.

"Um, Javase, where do you think you would like to eat?"

"Thank you for coming, Mr. Selvitz. I needed a friend to unload on and I know you are so caring and understanding with LeeAnn. You are saving my life. If you don't mind driving a little so we can have time to talk, I'd like to go somewhere out of town. Besides you are so famous here in town that everyone knows you. I've always heard that the James House in Sioux City has wonderful food. Is that too far?"

"Good choice, I love the food there. LeeAnn's mother won't travel that far to eat, but they have a dynamite chef. Sounds like an adventure. If we're going out of town, you better scrunch down in that seat, so everyone doesn't see me driving you away."

"Of course," she said, "What was I thinking?"

She unbuckled, pulled her flats off, and nestling her head in her left arm, she lay down with her left arm in his lap, her hand was brushing his right thigh, her head lay on his leg. She pulled her feet up on the seat and relaxed.

"I love your Caddy. Look it's so big I can lay down. Is this okay? Can I be seen like this?"

"You're okay there. LeeAnn used to sleep like that on trips."

"Drive careful, I'm unbuckled."

George reached into the backseat, careful not to disturb her head, and picked up a lap blanket. He spread it carefully over her.

She would be warmer and if he kept watching her legs, he was going to end up in a ditch. He drove slowly and carefully. At ten miles down the road, he said, "It's okay if you want to sit up now." She didn't move, must have gone to sleep. The feeling of her elbow in his lap gently rubbing against him with the rocking of the old tar road had him as excited as he could ever remember.

Javase, still awake, could feel his excitement. She snuggled in a little closer, moving her arm so it rubbed a little more fully against him.

He shook her shoulder to wake her up. "We're getting close now, you better sit up."

She sat up with a start. "I'm sorry. I must have fallen asleep. Everything was so comfortable and safe. I better comb my hair and get ready to eat." She reached into her purse and pulled out a pair of black slacks which she pulled on under her skirt. Undid the skirt's zipper and buttons and peeled it off down over the slacks. She pushed her feet into a pair of low heels, then reached back into her purse, and took out her make-up.

Ah ha, thought George watching her in the mirror as she twisted around getting dressed - orange panties.

She opened her mirror and began applying heavy dark make-up to her eyes. "Makes me look older, don't you think?" When they got out of the car and Javase shook her hair, and straightened her clothes, he had to agree. She looked to be in her mid-twenties. The maître' d did not even look twice when he seated them in the formal dining room. They were in a full booth meant for 6 people. When he sat at one side, thinking she would sit across from him, she sat on the edge of the booth next to him and scooched in until they were thigh to thigh. At first he was uncomfortable with her that close, but she began to prattle away about her classes and friends in school: the teachers and counselors in her school who were never understanding. He began to see that she was, after all, only fourteen and had no clue about her effect on him. When the waiter came, with the mandatory towel over one arm, he was surprised when she ordered a martini, straight up, with Boodles gin and an olive. The waiter asked for identification and she handed him a driver's license with her picture, saying she was twenty-two. He ordered a double scotch on the rocks. "Got it from The Toronto Free Press. It wouldn't fool the patrolmen, but it works on bartenders who really want to serve you anyway."

As they sipped their drinks, she showed George her fingernails which she had painted a light shade of red. "It's harder than you would think to keep them looking nice. Men have so many things that they don't have to fuss with. Holding both hands in front of her, she asked him, "Don't you think I have pretty hands? I think they are my best feature." She bent one nail over and it straightened back up. "My nails are so healthy. I eat a lot of protein and it keeps them strong."

George was looking at her hands but thinking about the leg touching his. She ordered a filet and a glass of house burgundy. He ordered a porterhouse and wine also. She did exhibit a healthy appetite. She had said she was hungry. She attacked the steak, ignored the salad and potato, pushed the plates away, finished her wine, and held up one imperious hand to order another glass. The waiter was obviously watching her and quickly brought another glass of burgundy.

She settled back against the booth, relaxing, resting her head on his shoulder.

"Thank you so much. Just a friendly face and an hour or two away from that madhouse means the world to me. You have helped me so much."

George was still working on his porterhouse, but he turned to look at the top of her head. "No problem, Javase, I always have time to help a friend of LeeAnn's. She has a constant battle going with her mother, it can be a real madhouse, like you said." He pushed his plate away, his steak was too big. No doggie bags today.

"If you're finished, I'll have it," she said, pointing at his steak.

"You can certainly have it, but I've been eating on it."

Javase rose slightly, turned her head and kissed him on the mouth. "You can be so funny sometimes, George. Now we have the same germs." She pulled his steak over and began eating.

He was stunned. He had no idea what to do next. He watched her quietly eat.

Javase, her mouth full of steak, turned to look deeply into his eyes, at the same time she reached for her wine. Her hand managed to hit only the top lip and the wine glass bounced and poured the full contents of red wine into George's lap.

"Oh dear," she said, "I am so clumsy." She started to wipe at the wine in his lap with her napkin.

He quickly pushed her hands away. "I'll go to the restroom and rinse these pants out. I'll be back in a moment."

"Mr. Selvitz, you'll look terrible. Why don't you just rent a room for the afternoon. That way you can rinse all your clothes out. They have an iron, I'll help you iron them, you'll look so much better. You can even take a shower if you want to."

"That is such an excellent idea, Javase. Excuse me while I go get a room."

"Mr. Selvitz, my parents stayed in room 314 on their honeymoon. Do you think you could get that room?"

"I'm sure I can. Sweetie, why don't you head up there? I'll meet you in five minutes."

George opened the room for her. She walked in going right to the television and turned it on. She went to the small refrigerator and pulled out a soft drink and sat before the set in an easy chair.

He sat on the edge of the bed, removed his shoes and socks, took hangers from the closet and walked into the bathroom. Clothes washed, and hung up, he put on the robe and returned to the closet to set up the ironing board and plug in the iron. He looked over at Javase, who now was lying in the middle of the bed with an open bottle of vodka in her hand. An emptied bottle laid by her chair.

Christ, he thought, how am I going to get her sober before I get her home? Hope Dan doesn't try to kill me. If I can get her out to the car still walking, she'll have an hour of fresh air to help her. He took off his robe and stood under the water as hot as he could take it. What an afternoon. The shampoo and soap smelled pleasant. He heard the door open, then close, as he pulled the curtain back, Javase stepped into the shower with him.

"Surprise, I thought I might need a shower too." She pulled his head down to her and kissed him deeply. "I always thought you would have a beautiful body."

No sense in trying to hide his excitement from her now. In twenty years, Penny Ann had never gotten into a shower with him or told him he had a beautiful body.

"That's enough showering, come with me." She took him by the hand and headed back to the bed, which was stripped to the sheets now. The blankets were bunched on the floor at the foot of the bed.

She jumped to the middle of the bed and lay spread out with her head on a pillow. George just stood for a minute looking. She was the most exotically beautiful thing he had ever seen. Her skin was the color of mocha latte. He thought he would love to start every day with a cup of Javase. He sat on the edge of the bed and reached for her.

"Let's start with a happy meal," she said, pulling his head down between her breasts. He felt, he looked, he tasted, but she was pushing his head down further. Between her legs now he breathed in the deep earthy odor. Then tasted her for the first time. He was twisted around trying to take the pressure off his erection. Javase, giggling a little, said, "Move that bad boy up here. I want to get a closer look at him. Maybe I can help you a little."

He knew she was responding to his hands and tongue, but he felt her take hold of him the first time and almost exploded. She rubbed him on her face, then licked him once and took him into her mouth. He could no longer wait and came hard. He continued to work on her with his hands and tongue until he felt her spasm and come in his mouth.

He flipped around and rested his head on the pillow next to hers. They kissed and held each other. Soon he felt her hand beginning to work magic with him.

"I'm certainly ready to feel something large and hard inside me."

He entered her slowly, she was so tight. Once fully inside, they began the slow dance. Feeling each other's body while slowly moving their hips. All dances end and this one ended with a mutual climax. They held tight through the spasms. "That was divine," said George.

Later, on their way out through the hotel lobby, George took Javase into the jewelry story attached, and bought her a Guess watch. It's brilliance on her wrist made her eyes shine.

"Something to help you remember the best of times."

He remembered it as the afternoon of bliss. The day when his sexual fantasies came true. She was the most beautiful thing he had ever seen with her luscious lips and nubile body. Perhaps he could live out the rest of his life with Penny Ann knowing that at least once his dreams had come true. Perhaps somehow, he could arrange another afternoon with Javase.

Then on the tenth day, he received the envelope. The pictures were so different than what he remembered. The pictures showed an old man abusing a small young girl. She was posing. Her face was so clear in each picture. She was obviously being raped from the pain on her face. The letter demanded $5000 in used bills.

How could he have been so stupid? She picked the place and the room and he had gone like a blind fool. The room must have been set up previously. How many times had she pulled a scam like this? There must be some way out. He worked on the problem most of the night. He ended up sending the money out in the morning. There was no escape. He been caught like a catfish sucking a rancid worm.

16
The Gambler

FRANK LEFT EARLY for work, while D'Angelo and I made breakfast and sat talking over our coffee. He called me around ten from his office. He had talked to Deputy Johnson, who told him he was in Vermillion when he heard the 911 call go out, and since there was a local man killed, he went down to check it out. He went to the hospital to see if he could identify the injured man. His story was copacetic on the face of it.

"Want to go out to see Janet and Al with me?"

The rain was still falling, so I put on a cap and jacket and waited near the front door. When he showed up, we drove out to their farm, and parked in front of the machine shop door.

"Watch your step here, Frank, she's shot at least two people already."

"Got my jacket on, it'll stop her bullets if she shoots."

He stood to the side of the door frame when he knocked. No answer. He knocked again, louder. Still no answer. He pushed the door open, and stepped back. No movement at all. He stepped into the kitchen. Saw Al's body lying motionless, appearing to be dead. The smell of blood and dead bodies permeated the air.

He came back to stand by me at the car. "I think they're both dead. I could see Al's body. I'm going to have to call in state forensics."

He made a call on his cell phone to Rosa, told her to contact them, and direct them to Al and Janet's farm. He pulled on shoe covers, left his hat on, and went back to the house. Five minutes later, he was out talking to me again.

"They're both dead, safe is open and empty. Looks to me like someone broke in, made Janet open the safe, then killed them both. I have to tape the area off until forensics finishes. They have a dozen doughnuts in there, but everything stinks. Feel like driving back into town to get us some doughnuts and coffee? I have to wait here."

"Sure," I say, "it'll make me feel like a real policeman."

We finished the doughnuts and coffee before the Department of Criminal Investigation guys showed up. We were sitting and smoking a cigar inside the garage, out of the rain, when the SUVs and cars showed up.

Fast and efficient, they donned head covers, shoe covers, and gloves were put on, and they entered the farmhouse. Photographing and marking evidence, they certainly were professional.

Ten minutes later, they came out with astounding news: two people dead, looks like a robbery. "They are bundling up the bodies now and fingerprinting the place. Leave the tape in place for a couple of days, in case they find anything on the bodies or the fingerprints provides us with more evidence."

Frank and I return to town. He has to find their next of kin and notify them. I watch a little television with D'Angelo. Frank came back late in the afternoon. The City Council had an emergency meeting with him. Several of the deputies had complained about the questioning and the Council wanted answers. Their town now had three killings and a robbery while he was wasting the deputies time about an investigation that was finished? They sweated him for several hours. Essentially, he was told to drop the crap or someone else would be acting sheriff, and the acting sheriff would have a large step up on being elected.

"You must be getting on someone's nerves. He's getting crowded by your actions."

"I'm not too sure what I should do now. I've listened to your accounts, but the state has also put a lot of time in investigating. They are professionals and know what they're doing. It's a problem that could blow up on me. I'm having a difficult time finding an answer."

"The answer, Frank, is you. You are the problem. It's just that you don't want to come to terms with it. I saw the tells when I came. You're not sleeping good, up all night, smoking rate has doubled, losing weight, and having no appetite. You knew the truth and swallowed the lie.

"The Department of Criminal Investigation gave you a song and dance about John's guilt and you went along, because they were the so-called professionals. If you had stood tall, and acted on the truth as you knew it, John would probably still be alive. DCI and that coroner served you up an easy answer. It was a load of crap, but you took the easy way. Now you gotta decide: easy way and promotion, or hard way and the truth."

"Damn, Matt," said Frank, "Don't sugar coat it. Nice to know you think I'm the problem. For the last five days, I've been thinking you're the problem, you contrary bastard. It's not like I haven't been doing my best."

"Me? You think it's me, the one who is not working the investigation? That's a real laugh, Frank."

"Look at what you've done for me so far, Matt. You convinced me that John wasn't the killer, so I upset the whole department and the City Council trying to prove the unprovable. Now you want me to prove that Margo and John's death was a double homicide. I go from having a clean slate, to having three unsolved murders. You keep investigating, this town will end up the murder capital of the west, and I'll go down as the worst sheriff ever."

"Frank, the people of Tindale don't believe we can catch this guy. I know we can, but you have to be aboard. I came too close to being croaked already. Your knowledge of the people and the town are crucial, as they should be to a sheriff."

"What in tarnation would make you believe I am not with you all the way? I don't really give a damn whether I am sheriff or not. I feel more like chucking this job and becoming a pro gambler like you. I'm telling you, the crap I'm going through daily is just not worth the money. You can carry some of it too. Now, let's go find these brothers from Avon."

Rosa located a family that lived near Avon which still had two adult sons living at home. Frank called the father, a man named Arvin Burns. He said he would meet us at the café in Avon, at three in the afternoon.

"I appreciate your coming in to talk to me," I said, as I stirred a packet of creamer into my coffee. I am not overly fond of the stuff, but it gave me something to do instead of making the guy nervous by looking at him too hard. He was dressed as a farmer. He had worn bib-overalls covering a blue chambray shirt. His shirt was buttoned up to his neck and at the sleeves, a green John Deere hat remained on his head, a wedding ring was on his left hand, and he had a cheap Timex watch on his wrist.

"I understand your two adult sons both live at home with you."

"Are those two knot heads in trouble again?"

"No," I said, "I just wanted to talk to them about a fight they got into in Tindale, last week."

"They get into a lot of fights. You'd think they would grow up a little, but might just as well talk to a tree as talk to them."

"Yeah," I replied, "the young people today don't listen to us much. Do you think they would come in to talk to me; that is, if it's okay with you?"

"Of course, it's okay with me, and I think they would come in, but they are in Las Vegas. Been there a week now and plan on staying for another week or two. I'm only surprised the two bums didn't wait until spring planting came before they took off."

17
Javase

IT WAS A bad night for Javase. She had picked up the envelope that afternoon. In her room, she had rapidly counted through the money twice. $5000. Fifty one hundred dollar bills. Money beyond which she had ever dreamed. Plans are plans, but holding the money was exhilarating. She bagged the money into Ziplocs and buried them in the backyard sandbox. The kids hadn't played in it for years now. It sat abandoned and deteriorating, surrounded by weeds. Her escape was so close. Hard to remain calm.

She had two glasses from the bourbon bottle her parents had stashed in the cupboard over the refrigerator. They were certain it would never be found there. Most of the night she had lain awake, making plans, preparing for her escape. She had a few clothes and a jacket in her backpack, now hidden under her bed. She wanted to be up early before anyone knew she was gone; she could be on the road to Sioux Falls or Sioux City. She would hitch to either depending on where the driver was heading. Then a bus ride to New York. Everything great happens in New York. Within months she was sure she would be a headliner.

Plans began going south when she overslept. The kids were running around. She helped them get dressed, cooked oatmeal for them, and was getting them ready to head off to school when her father offered to drive them. She'd gone in the front door and out the back. Walked up two blocks to where she could watch the sheriff's office, and when her father pulled in for work, she began a quick jog for home. Her mother's car was gone, probably off shopping. She dug up the money first, packed it into her backpack with her clothes and left for the highway. Goodbye forever to this losing family. She wouldn't miss them.

The first two vehicles didn't pick her up. An eighteen-wheeler who probably had rules against riders and an older farmer who probably didn't even see her. The third car was her father. He pulled over and through the open window called to her. "Where you headed for Javase? Thought I just dropped you at school."

"I was heading in to shop at Yankton Mall. I wanted to get a new teddy and some great perfume as a treat for you."

"That would be nice, but I don't have anything this morning. Let's go to our special place. I'll drive you to Yankton for shopping and food later."

Fear shot through her. Something in the timbre of his voice was not right. She glanced about, what could she do? Nowhere to run to. No way out. She threw her pack into the backseat, crawled in the front, and buckled up.

That sounds great. I've been missing our special times," she said, smiling her sweetest innocent smile.

He spent several hours with her at their special place, an abandoned farm house six miles out of town. He had painted an upstairs bedroom and decorated it with frilly touches. The power and water had been turned on, so the room could be used any time. When the heavy curtains were pulled, no lights could be seen from outside. This was the room they had used for the pictures with Melanie and Pastor John.

That had been a long afternoon with the two men watching her and Melanie. First just taking pictures, then joining them.

Now for the first time, she saw her father was using a condom. He had bottles of the morning after pills, so why the condoms? Even stranger, he was uninterested in oral sex. He had always been wild for it before. He's getting too weird, she thought. Footsteps on the stairs were not a welcome sound.

"He's giving us a couple of hundred for an hour alone with you. Be nice, okay? Maybe we'll even shop for a car this afternoon."

"Hey, John, come in. We were wondering if you would make it out today. I'm going down for a smoke," he said, "Leave you two alone for a while."

"Hey Johnny," Javase said, "I hear you've been a bad boy. Take that jacket off and come sit by me."

Dan was still down below when John came out and they talked for a few minutes. John gave him an envelope filled with money, "She was wonderful today, but it's getting harder to find the money."

"You'll think of something, John. You are very resourceful. Hey, you know anything about guns? I just got this little pistol as my backup. You like it?" He put his Beretta Tomcat in John's hand. "Light, isn't it? Has a good feel, don't you think?"

"I do like it. You say this is your backup piece?"

"Yeah, it's a little too light for a service pistol. Here, this is what I carry, a .38 police special. Heavier with more stopping power."

John hefted the two, looked them over, "I like the .38 better." He extended them both back to Dan, but he was lighting a cigarette and looking away down the road. Uncomfortable with them in his hands, John put them on the porch step.

"Better hit the road before Wifey gets suspicious. Thanks again for calling me."

As Pastor John drove down the lane toward the county road, Dan slipped on a pair of latex gloves, picked up the Tomcat and walked back upstairs. Javase was starting to dress as he came into the room.

"What's the hurry with you today? You know I love to watch you dress."

She smiled at him, "No problem." She reached behind her back and unfastened her bra.

Dan pushed her over to the bed. Forced her down with one hand, brought the Tomcat out from behind his back, and shot her under the chin. The bullet went up through her brain, killing her instantly. He dropped the gun onto the bed. No prints on it but John's. No DNA in her but John's.

"Oh Javase," he said looking at her body. "I'll never find another one like you. Too bad you grew up and got so smart. You were a fire-cracker at ten and did nothing but get hotter. Thanks for the extra money." He wiped down all the places he could remember touch-ing. He had wiped the place down the night before so it should be clean. Everything in the house had been purchased by Ed Mathews. The same guy had turned on the lights and water. As far as Dan could see, he was in the clear for everything here. He picked up the .38, put it in his belt holster, got in his car and one mile down the road, peeled off his gloves and threw them out the window.

He was home again by two. Sat with his wife and had lunch. A grilled cheese sandwich with a thick slice of tomato and mustard in it. One of his favorite sandwiches. He was talking with Silvia about the kids, when she noticed the blood stain on the arm of his shirt.

"Oh, Danny, what happened to your arm?"

"Scratched it on a pickup truck I was searching this morning. After lunch, I'm going to the clinic for a dressing and a typhus shot. Real pain in the ass." He gave a low chuckle. "What did you buy in Yankton?"

"Bought a new dress for church, come in and I'll try it on for you."

As she walked through the bedroom door, he hit her with his billy on the back of her head. She crumpled, appearing lifeless. He hit her several more times to make sure. He dragged her body all the way into the bedroom and laid her out at the foot of the bed. He rolled up his sleeve and saw the long scratches Javase had inflicted on him in her struggle. He washed, and dressed the wounds, cursing his luck. No time now to go out and clean under her fingernails. No problem really. He was going to be gone. He went to his car, opened the trunk and carried the body he had stashed there into the house and laid it on the bed. He had picked a homeless man close to his size and shape, who had been panhandling in Sioux Falls. He undressed him, then took off his uniform and put it on the man. He rolled him over several times until the body fell next to his wife. He picked up his service pistol, and muffling the shots with pillows, put a round into the heads of both bodies. From his shed, he brought in two one gallon cans of fuel oil, and three cans of hairspray he had purchased right after he had killed the man in Sioux Falls.

Sitting at the table with a beer, he waited for the kids to come home from school. He was quick this time, no shots, only his club. He left their bodies where they fell. He carried one can of fuel oil into the bedroom and poured it over the two bodies. He poured out the other can in the kitchen, making sure the stove was covered. He placed two cans of hairspray on the stove's top, the other can he put on his wife's dresser in the bedroom. He lit a small birthday candle, stuck it between his wife's fingers. He lit another candle and placed it upright on the floor near the stove, and walked out the back door quickly. He walked slowly down the street to where he parked his real car, a used Beamer, he'd bought used several years ago in Chicago. As he started the engine, he could see the smoke pouring from the house. An hour later he was in his apartment in Mitchell. He'd rented it under the name of Cyrus Cobb. He would be safe here, but he knew soon someone would recognize him. He packed up all the treasures he had been storing here: rare coins, gold bullion, cash, and a closet full of great clothes. The money from Javase, Melanie, and the two boys of John's had been more than he had believed possible. He had married Silvia planning an insurance scam when he killed her and her kids. But Javase had changed his mind. She had always been a hot little number. If he hadn't put his hand down her pants to help her along one afternoon, the four of them would have already been dead, and he would be living somewhere with a new identity and a stack of insurance money. Being male, he couldn't believe a ten year old girl would be that enthusiastic for sex, but as he came to terms with his new step daughter, new plans for making money developed.

Now he had the additional $5000 that Javase had in her backpack, plus the pictures of her with George Selvitz. She had been an enterprising little wench. What he had shown her, she had quickly learned.

By the time the fire had been extinguished and the charred bodies found, he was sitting in the Mount Vernon Inn, eating a blackened steak. He heard about his death on channel 5 out of Sioux Falls. Nice to know the police would be searching for his killer. Two slow beers later, he was back in the BMW heading to Tindale. It was after midnight when he pulled up in front of Pastor John's. He put his gloves back on, picked up his service pistol, and put it under the front seat of John's car. Have to love small town America where few lock their cars. He picked up Interstate 29 north, then I-90 west. Time to see what life could be like in the west. Colorado here I come.

18
The Fire

THE DARK ORANGE and yellow flames ate through the old building rapidly sending black billowing clouds into the afternoon sky. The Volunteer Fire Department immediately put in calls for assistance to the nearby towns. There were several loud blasts as cans inside the house exploded. Hoses unwound, the firemen wet down the nearby houses, sent word to gas company to shut down the fuel to the house, then aimed the water at the flames. There was no saving the house, the fire was too advanced, but they kept the water on it to subdue the flames. Finally beating it down to a smoldering heap, the leading team entered the house to kill the hot spots still burning. They found the bodies right away in the kitchen. As per procedure, the call went out to the state fire marshal.

The evidence quickly convinced the fire marshal that the fire had been arson. Therefore, the bodies were listed as probable homicides. DCI soon arrived and the investigation began.

Frank saw the TV lights from down the street. The cute blonde lady from Channel Five was holding a microphone in front of the fire marshal, who looked at ease while he dodged their questions.

Frank could see three other cameramen with portable lights roaming the area of the burned house, filming the disaster, and looking for a good place to set up their lights.

Damn, he thought, just the extra push the City Council will need to get rid of me. This will be a full three ring circus and I'm set up to be the head clown.

As Frank approached the fire marshal, they flooded him with light and stuck a microphone in front of him. "No comment," he said, "This is an ongoing investigation. Wait until I touch base with the fire marshal and DCI, maybe then I will have something for you."

He approached one of the DCI men that he knew from previous work. "How bad does it look, Larry?"

"Bad as it can be, Frank. There are two adults, a man and a woman, the male was dressed in a deputy's uniform, both have been shot in the head. There are two children in there also. No cause of death has been established for them, as yet, but you can rest assured they were murdered too. The cause of death will be established tomorrow by the medical examiner. We'll have him rush it tonight."

"This is the house of Deputy Dan Johnson. He is married and has three children. The bodies will probably be Officer Johnson, his wife Silvia, and their two boys. He also has a teenage daughter, so it's probable that there is another body in there somewhere."

"We'll be working through the night, scraping through all this. Will let you know if we find anything else. By the way, it was definitely arson, an accelerant was used."

As he left the area, he was again surrounded by the TV crew. "The preliminary investigation has revealed at least four bodies. Nothing more can be said until the next of kin are notified. This was a horrendous crime and our department will not stop until the perpetrator is arrested."

19
Javase

FRANK WAS EXHAUSTED when he arrived home. The forms he needed to complete were myriad. The governor had called and talked to him. He had found a next of kin for Silvia, but nothing for Dan. He had notified Silvia's mother of the deaths and that a search was on for Javase.

The message light was blinking on his phone when he finally sat down at the kitchen table with a shot of bourbon and a cold beer. He stared at it. I don't care who it is or what they want. He swallowed the bourbon in one gulp, chased the burn with cool beer, and went back to looking at the light.

"This job sucks." He pushed the blinking light.

In less than an hour, he was looking at the body of Javase.

Ten minutes later, six cars pulled into the farm lot and DCI began their forensic work.

20
John

THE 911 CALL came in at 8:25 that evening. The man on the line reported, in a frightened western drawl, that he had seen Pastor John driving in an erratic manner, waving a gun out of his window. Rosa had taken the message and notified acting Sheriff Frank Smith immediately.

Sheriff Smith had Deputy Daniels begin a sweep down Main Street, looking for John's older Chevy, while he jumped in his patrol car and drove down past the Church of Christ the Savior. He saw Pastor John pulling away from the church's parking lot. He turned on his lights, pulling the car over to the side of the road. Surprised, John rolled down his window, thinking maybe that Frank wanted to talk to him about something.

"What's the problem, Frank? Do I have a light out?"

"Good evening, sir. I'm Sheriff Frank Smith. Please let me see your driver's license, insurance card, and registration."

"Are you kidding, Frank? What kind of law did I break?"

"Your driver's license, insurance, and registration, please."

Pastor John's anxiety began to rise. He could feel that something serious was happening. He began to dig around in his glove compartment searching for the documents. Finding them, he handed the cards to Frank.

"Do you have any open containers, drugs, or weapons in your vehicle?"

"Certainly not. I don't even have a gun. I just finished my sermon at the church."

John opened the door, stood, and walked toward the front of the car.

"Do I have your permission to search the vehicle?"

"Certainly, Frank. You know perfectly well that I don't have any open containers."

Frank took out his flashlight, looked into the front seat, then the back, then leaning over, he shone the light under the front seat and saw the butt of a pistol.

"John, there is a pistol under your front seat. I'm going to have to cuff you. Please put your hands behind your back."

After he was cuffed, Frank asked him if he had any weapons on his person.

"Certainly not. I told you, I don't even own a gun."

Frank frisked him quickly, found nothing, then told John to wait while he made a call. He radioed in to Rosa, code 1054, request for backup, took out his camera and an evidence bag, and waited for backup. When Deputy Daniels arrived, he explained the situation quickly. He pulled on gloves, took pictures of the gun while it was still under the seat, then pulled it out, laid it on the floorboards, and took another picture. He looked again under the seat, saw another gun, photographed it, pulled it out, and took another picture of the two weapons. He put the guns into an evidence bag and sealed it.

John's face registered surprise. He thought he recognized the two pistols as the ones Deputy Johnson had shown him. Why would Johnson put them under his front seat? This had to be a setup of some kind, but why he wondered. Frank searched the rest of the car, and found three pieces of jewelry in the glove compartment. He photographed them, put the jewelry in a separate evidence bag, took the keys, opened and searched the trunk. Under the spare tire, he found the yellow envelope with the pictures of Javase, Melanie, and John's two sons inside.

"Damn, what kind of sick bastard takes naked pictures of his own kids?" said Deputy Daniels.

"It's hard to believe," said Frank, "But those pictures will be golden for getting him put away. Arrange a tow for his car, will you? Have them park it behind the jail, then wrap evidence tape around it."

He called Rosa at the office, told her what happened, and then drove John to the jail and sat him down in the chair across from his desk. When Daniels came in, they read John his rights.

"Do you understand your rights as I've explained them?"

"Yes."

"Do you want to tell me how those pictures got in your car?"

"I don't want to say anything until I've talked to my lawyer. Can I make my phone call?"

"Not quite yet."

Frank called Rosa. "What judge is on tonight and where is he? We need to get a search warrant before any evidence is destroyed."

Ten minutes later, he and Daniels were at John's house. Melanie screamed at them as they searched the house, finding nothing else to incriminate John. They took his computer, video equipment, and their cell phones.

He gave John his phone call when he returned to the jail. The next morning he had John before the judge. Bond was set at $500,000, and John was transferred to the jail at Mitchell pending the results of the investigation. The evidence was boxed and sent by express mail to DCI the next morning.

21
Matt

ON THE WHOLE, I am unhappy with my actions over the last two weeks. Looking at too many situations at once blurred the edges of each. It was so easy to believe John was the killer and wrap up the killing with neat red ribbons and bows. Why had I placed a bet with Sherry? Why had I agreed to go to her poker party? This was no time to feed the beast or spend the evening involving my brain in sense-less activity to avoid the tough mental sweat needed to break this conundrum and catch the killer.

After dressing in the dark, I walk in stocking feet to the kitchen. Turning on the lights and cold water, I put three scoops of coffee into the basket, fill the maker with water and turn it on, and reach for a glass. A full glass of cold water every morning helps my brain begin to function better. Filling a large mug with steaming coffee, I grab my cigars, open the back door, and step into the cool morning air. I sit in a plastic banded lawn chair, and set the mug on the deck. I lean back, tear the top of the cigar pack off with my teeth, light a cigarillo, and look up at the stars.

Perhaps a little ancient light fired straight from a distant star will clear my fog-filled brain.

Everything points to Reverend John. Everyone thinks it's Pastor John. He was alone when Sluggo had been killed, allegedly working on his Sunday evening service at the church. The vaginal DNA evidence proves the rape of Javase. His fingerprints on the two pistols are strong forensic evidence that he killed Al, Janet, and Javase.

As to Sluggo's death, John Thurman had the time, but would he have had the knowledge necessary to accomplish it? When could he ever have been in the jail? How would he know where the keys were kept? Plus, he was not Slug's friend. How did he get close enough to kill him without Slug fighting back? It's not an easy thing to break someone's neck. Thurman does not look strong enough to have killed Slug that way.

The evidence makes me believe that only with outlandish luck could John have succeeded in killing Slug. As a gambler, I am skeptical of outlandish luck. In the investigation thus far, I have recognized meticulous planning and organization. Luck has not played a part. The DNA found in Javase and the presence of the kiddie porn prove that John is guilty of at least rape, but statutory rape and kiddie porn do not equate with murder. Also, the DNA taken from under Javase's fingernails doesn't match up with Thurman. That certainly seems to point to a different killer, although the pistol still points to John. The insurance agent confirmed that the jewelry recovered in Thurman's car was, in fact, Janet's. So Al and Janet's death is connected to Thurman.

No question. The pistol being found under his car seat certainly seems to tie him to the couple's death.

That evidence would be more damning to me if it had not been found so easily. Thurman is not stupid. In today's world, everyone knows about forensic evidence. Any man committing a murder knows he must get rid of the evidence. Why had Thurman not tossed the guns and jewelry into the Missouri from the top of the bridge? The answer is too obvious, he had not known the evidence was under his front seat. It had been planted on him by the real killer.

Where is the rest of the loot from the safe? Janet would have had many more pieces of jewelry in that safe. Plus, there would have been money. I think they hoarded lots of money. Perhaps Frank can get the list of jewelry from the insurance company and see if any has been pawned.

Who is the killer? If I eliminate John, that only leaves three deputies, none of whom I believe could be the killer. The call from Deadwood the night after the fire is the answer. Who called? It's possible that the killer called a friend and had him report it. But that would involve a second conspirator. Unlikely that it wouldn't have been planned. So far there had been no loose strings, the death of Deputy Johnson had closed off all other avenues of investigation. My cigar a butt, the mug empty, I returned to the kitchen, refilled the cup and sat staring at it. The same thoughts kept swirling round and round leading to the same foggy mist: many questions and no answers.

Was it fear muddling up my thinking? I knew I was a target here. In the land of high powered rifles, any open space is an invitation to violent sudden death. Deep inside where I cannot avoid facing the truth, I know my fear is not going down with a 30.06 bullet tearing through my head. After years of being alone I find that here in this small town on the heart of the prairie, with a dangerous killer on the loose, I am no longer alone. If I die here now, at least three people care enough to come to my funeral. I know that with my actions, I will somehow turn everyone against me and everyone will leave. I see myself dying alone, crying in the dark. Nothing left to do now but dive into the fray.

D'Angelo came into the light followed by the sound of rapidly clicking toenails. He poured out a mug and sat across from me. Both dogs lay at his feet.

"Bad night?"

"Yeah, been running the last two weeks through my head and simply cannot accept that John is the perpetrator. Something doesn't add up. I'm stuck on the first guy's death. I believe that it's going to be the answer to this thing."

"Sounds like one of them old black and white movies where someone is not who he says he is. You know the one I mean, something like *Ten Little Indians*?"

"Yep, that's the name of it. You're right, this is a puzzler just like that was."

"Well it seems easy enough for you then. All you gotta do is figure out who isn't what he was, when he wasn't who he said he was. Piece of cake for the sleuth."

"D'Angelo," I said, "thanks for clearing that up for me. Any chance you got your papers handy?"

"I'll get them," he says, heading for his bag in the living room. "What's up?"

"Let's go look at a vehicle."

We walked to the local used car dealer. Not much in his lot but old sedans, beat-up pickup trucks, and one four-door Jeep about ten years old. I stood watching him, while D'Angelo looked at and got into them all, admiring each with enthusiasm.

The owner of the lot came out and stood beside me. I recognized him from the funeral, but couldn't remember his name. We talked about the weather. I lit a cigar and together we watched D'Angelo enjoying himself. I explained my situation. I wanted to rent one of the cars until my insurance check came.

"No problem," he says. "which one are you interested in?"

"The Jeep. What are you asking?"

He gave me a rather high figure which I immediately ignored.

"I'll give you five hundred cash to use it until my insurance check comes. Then if I like it, I'll just sign the check over to you."

"Let's get the paperwork done," he said, walking to his office.

We shook hands, then signed the insurance forms. God knows I love small towns and honest trusting people.

D'Angelo and I walked around our new Jeep. It was forest green with a few small dents and dings. The tires looked pretty good. I checked the oil, also showing D'Angelo how to do it, as he had not been around autos. The previous owner had upgraded the floor mats and mirrors, presenting a nice looking vehicle.

I got in the driver's seat, racked it all the way back, adjusted the mirrors, and clicked on the seat belt. I turned on the radio to make sure it worked, then shut it off.

"I want to hear the car running this first trip." We had half a tank of gas, so I headed out to the highway.

I drove to the highway, parked on the side of the road, and told D'Angelo it was time for him to have his first driving lesson. Shining Eyes and I changed places. He checked out the mirrors, adjusted the seat, and off we went.

I didn't tell him much; just reminded him to watch for farm machinery as it always moves slowly and to watch for deer and cows as they love getting on the road.

He took us down the road to Yankton, starting off pretty slow, but gradually working it up to fifty. There wasn't much along the highway but gently rolling hills, mailboxes, and farm sites. Looked like more than half of the houses had been abandoned; seemed like corporate farmers were entrenching themselves further into the heartland every day. D'Angelo did a good job for the first time behind a wheel. Once we hit the outskirts of Yankton, I reminded him to watch for kids and bad drivers.

"Don't get impatient. Just let them go first, and if you get puzzled, pull over to the side and stop."

"I'm watching," he said.

We pulled into the mall on the west end of town and parked.

"Wow, this baby handles great. Good choice, Matt."

"You think it's nice now, wait till we get it loaded down with camping and fishing gear. Be room for the doggies in here too."

In the mall, we searched out the Social Security office. We sat in the waiting area until a pretty older lady called us to her desk. Name on her desk was Pat Steckleberg. I told her D'Angelo was here to get his first Social Security card. Her attention jumped right to him. She pulled out a form, helped him fill it out, looked over his papers, and flashed him a smile. "Now all you have to do is sign it. I'll rush this through for you, Mr. Johnson, and it will come in the mail to you in less than a week."

He was pretty quiet when we left the office.

"You okay?"

"I am feeling like a real citizen for the first time. You know Matt, with a driver's license and Social Security card, there's really nothing in this country you can't do. I'm thinking the sky is the limit. This is the same way Bush and Clinton and Obama started. You never know how far you can go, someday maybe I'll run for president."

"Before you do that, how about we celebrate here at the Dairy Queen with a banana split?"

Before we left Yankton, I swung into a sporting store and bought a tent and a couple of air mattresses. They were having a sale on their used bikes also, so I bought a Giant road bike for D'Angelo.

On the way back to Tindale, I had D'Angelo pull into Sam Kelley's place. The gravel tracks were still visible, but the grass had grown high in the swale and brushed against the undercarriage. It worried D'Angelo a little, but we made it up to the house and parked in front.

"This is the place I'm renting now. We can use it for a mail drop and store our extra gear here until we decide to use it. Frank's place is a little small and I don't want to crowd him more than we already have."

I walked to the front door and while I was looking for the right key, D'Angelo ran around the house, through the long weeds, and down into the apple trees. When he returned to the house, he was munching on one that looked to be almost ripe. He raced through the first floor, took the stairs three at a time, checked out the second floor, and sailed back down.

"This is a great place, Matt. Did you really rent it? Are we going to stay out here?"

I looked again at the old house. Most of the paint had peeled and fallen off, the porch was drooping, the grass was at least knee high, and many of the limbs had died and fallen off the tree. It had a large graveled area where Kelley still drove frequently as he used the barn, the garage, and the grain way. Certainly needed a lot of upkeep and not the kind of house I would choose to live in. Apparently, D'Angelo thought it was special.

"I had only planned on using it as a mail drop. It would take a lot of work to live out here, wouldn't it?"

"Looks great to me."

Deep inside, something churned at me. Old ugly house it may be, but the emotion it evoked in D'Angelo touched me like nothing had for a long time. New emotions tearing at me, I walked out onto the porch, away from D'Angelo, blinked back any tears that were trying to escape, and looked down at the lawn tangled with weeds and the apple trees loaded with harvest redness, trying to see it from his eyes.

"Hey, D'Angelo," I said, "how about if we just camp out here tonight? We can get the dogs and cook up something over a camp-fire. Be nice for a little quiet time."

"Yeah, I'm up for that. I'll get the mattresses unpacked and blown up, which room you want?"

"Take your pick, I'll take the other. I am going back into town to get some food and the dogs. Want to come, or wait here?"

"I'll mess around here, get everything set up. Look over there, Matt, there's a bird nest in that little bush by the corner."

"Isn't that cute? Wonder what kind of birds. Probably be back in the spring."

In town, I turned on the electricity, stopped at the grocery and picked up some franks, buns, chips, and a twelve pack of soda. I stopped at Frank's house, borrowed his card table and chairs, told him we would be gone for the night, loaded the puppies, and headed back to the farm.

When I pulled into the lane, I saw D'Angelo riding his bike in the farmyard. When I parked, he headed down the lane, circled at the highway, and raced back up the lane.

He was breathing hard with a big smile on his face and jumped off. "Great bike."

I opened the door for Bogie and Thunder and they were off like a shot. No looking it over slowly for these two. They bounced off D'Angelo as though to acknowledge that he was there, then ran half-way down the lane and back. Around the house they flew, then out to the barn and the grain way, stopping to smell things in their path. A few loud barks to let the wild animals around know that the new bosses of the place were there, and back to sit at D'Angelo's feet. He looked at me, and I agreed, they loved the place.

D'Angelo had been busy. He'd blown up the mattresses, taken the room that overlooked the field, then dragged a dead tree branch down for firewood. Together, we built a little fire on a grate he'd found behind the house. I cut a couple of fresh limbs.

"We doing it the old way tonight," I said.

I speared a frank and held it over the fire. D'Angelo, always quick when it comes to food, had his in the fire seconds behind me. I had forgotten to get any mustard or ketchup, but they still tasted great chased down by warm sodas. What with fending the puppies off with one hand, eating with the other, and watching the fire, we had a fine night.

I slept good on the air mattress: no pillow, no blanket, no problem. Later, when I used the restroom, I checked on D'Angelo, but his room was empty. I checked downstairs. Heard a noise on the porch and saw him sitting quietly.

"You okay?"

He turned away from me, wiped his face with his hand, and turned back. "Sorry if I woke you up, Matt."

"Old man's curse got me up, not you."

"Just sitting here thinking is all. You know I'm a street kid from the city and don't nothing ever bother me, but tonight, something changed just a little. For the first time in years, I thought about my mother. She'd probably hate it here, but I'd give anything just to have her with me, sitting on a porch, just looking out at the field there, with the wind moving everything just a little. Don't know why she couldn't have met a guy like you, stead of that shit she went with."

"I'm heading back up. Stay up long as you want, nothing happening tomorrow. Maybe we'll stay out here again if you like it." I was asleep two minutes later.

The sun was still weak in the eastern sky when I walked out on the porch and let the puppies run. I sat on the steps and just watched them. There's a special freedom dogs have the country. The smells, the distance they can run, and the fresh air all seem to delight them. D'Angelo came out and sat beside me.

"Big plans today?"

"Road trip to Vermillion. I have got to get started on figuring out this killer. You want to ride, or mess around here with the dogs?"

"If you'll be looking at some food, I'll ride. They was great hot dogs, but they don't last too long."

We swung through Tabor, a small Czech town on the way, and bought a bag of kolaches and coffee.

"Buckets, these are great."

"I know. Strange thing though, they are made with goose grease. Sounds bad, tastes great."

"Bring that goose grease right on. Damn, they are really good."

We walked through the University of South Dakota campus to their library. The librarian was easy to dislike. She was an intellectual snob with little time to waste on a raggedy man and a teenager. I waited patiently until she acknowledged my presence and directed me to the shelves holding the yearbooks. I begin searching to find the book that Larry Temple would be in. He looked to be thirty years old, so I started looking nine years back. I found his smiling face in the third book I looked through. His wife Sandra's picture was next to his.

I established that 'he is who he says he is' to my satisfaction anyway, so I began to look for D'Angelo. He was walking the shelves of the books having a great time reading the titles.

"Got a lot of good computer and history books here."

"Yeah, colleges have to stay current to be relevant in the world today."

We stopped at the Goodwill store in Yankton on the way back. We got kitchen stuff, especially a coffee pot and some mugs.

"Anything else we need, D'Angelo?"

He went to look around and it turns out we needed a couple dozen comic books, a few mystery novels, and a book on Windows.

"I was going to get an old cooler, but then I thought maybe we ought to turn on that old fridge in the kitchen. You never know, it might work. What where you looking up back there in the library?"

"I got to thinking that maybe one of these deputies is not who he says he is. I'm just checking their stories to make sure we haven't overlooked something. I'm giving it the *Ten Little Indians* scrutiny. Now I know that Larry and Sandy Temple looked exactly the same seven years ago. I knew Wyatt Daniels back in Emmetsburg. He was five or six years ahead of me and I doubt that he knew me, but I know he is who he says he is. Dan Johnson's dead, so there's not much to check there. I'm down to researching Larry Anders. If he checks out, I'll probably just let it go, and figure Pastor John and Al did it all."

"Maybe I can help you with that," said D'Angelo. "There's a program called Classmates has a lot of the yearbooks shown online. It'll cost you $25 but save a lot of leg work for you."

"Let's fire it up tonight. Get this leg behind me. Hey, D'Angelo, look ahead there, off to the left, see that JoDean's Steakhouse sign. What say we eat?"

"I'm always ready to eat."

Back at the house, D'Angelo fired up his computer and began to work his magic. Less than an hour later, he was showing me a picture of Anders in his high school yearbook. There was no question in my mind that it was him. The door on that line of search was closed. Where to begin looking now, or should I let the whole thing drop and go back to Chicago?

"I'm heading into town. Be back in a couple of hours."

D'Angelo had already picked up a comic as I left.

Sherry was behind the bar, and opened me a Bud as I walked in. "Nice to see you big guy. How's things with you?"

"Not much shaking here. Thinking of heading back to Windy for a while. Say, how's my tab doing here?"

"So if you are not that busy, why couldn't you have called me in the last couple of days? Could have at least let me know you're alive. Your tab is okay, you're still up a couple of hundred. Got a poker game later if you want to come."

"I can't make it tonight. I've got a lot to tell you, please forgive me for not calling earlier. You got any plans for tomorrow? I would like to make dinner for you at your place. Give you a chance to meet D'Angelo."

"I would love it Matt. I'll take off at four, if that will give you enough time."

"Count me in. Any ball games tonight?"

She gave me a list of the games, then gave me a slow look. "You know there ain't nothing happening in Chicago, and there's a lot still happening here. I know I would hate to see you leave so soon."

We made small talk for a while, I put two hundred on the Nationals, and drank a couple more Buds. I watched the Nats sink deeply into a deficit. Seems Hardin, their home run hitter had bad muscle spasms that night. Before I left, I gave Sherry twenty to cover the vig and I called it a night.

On the way home I stopped to talk to Frank, and told him about my wasted day of investigating. He was a little down anyway. The

City Council had questioned him about his use of the deputy's time. He'd been on the hot seat for better than an hour. He was still acting sheriff, but he knew that was dangling by a thin line.

"Damn, Frank, I didn't mean to cause you no harm. Seems ridiculous that you could be removed when you have Pastor Thurmond in jail with what looks to be insurmountable evidence."

"Councilman Burns is politicking for his nephew Steve Anders. Small towns can suck." "Crazy. I wish you the best with that. You know I don't believe you have the killer yet, but that Thurman should probably get the death penalty anyway. My question to you is, do you still want to go after the real killer?"

"Of course I do, Matt. I believe you're right. I just can't seem to find a way to pursue this any further. I hear those two farm boys are back from Vegas, so watch yourself. Want to go see them again?"

"Sure would. Make it early though, got plans tomorrow afternoon."

22
Melanie

MIRIAM, PASTOR JOHN'S wife, is dressed in a subdued blue dress that falls mid-calf and is buttoned at the neck. She is visibly uncomfortable sitting in the hard wooden chair in the interrogation room. She looks from Frank, to the window, down at the table, then back at Frank. Her answers are slow in coming, she is thinking over every word before she speaks. The recorder clearly has her upset. She is a tallish woman, carrying twenty to thirty extra pounds, her dull brown hair is cut short. She has remarkably small pretty hands, wide hips, and large breasts. She radiates an aura of subdued sensuality.

She brought her children with her to the interview, and they are waiting in another room for her to finish. She has two boys, Jeff and Joe, that look to be about fourteen. Both are thin, shy, and withdrawn. They stood close to Miriam when they were together, seeming to have no pockets to put their hands in. Miriam's daughter, Melanie, is seventeen. She's pretty with light brown hair. A little overweight, she also has wide hips and a full figure. Talking to her, her mental impairment is readily discerned. She talks and acts more like a second grader, than someone who should be getting ready to graduate.

"What do you want me to say?" Miriam asked.

"Just tell it like it was with you and John."

"We had a great marriage and I loved him totally. And then the bad times came because he was weak, but I still loved him. I want you to know it never seemed wrong when everything was happening. Looking back now, I know we were terrible parents. We did things wrong. But, John was my husband, he was head of the household, and I loved and believed in him. I still adore John with all my heart and I cannot believe he did the things you've charged him with.

"Everything between us changed one bad day when I came home early and he was giving her a bath. No father should be giving his twelve year old daughter a bath. There they were, laughing and talking, while he was shampooing her hair while she sat in the tub. She was just starting to become a woman. I could see her little breasts just starting to form. Coward that I was, I left and said nothing. I didn't want to believe what I saw cause our world would have come to an end. I know now that I should have protected her better. But she always seemed happy, like what was happening was normal. He saw me in the doorway watching them, and continued on bathing her. It was the real end of our marriage, such as it was. He no longer felt any passion for me. When we did make love, I could feel it was just a chore for him that he felt he had to do.

"The heat was gone between us. Soon he stopped coming to my bed. I was sure he was sleeping with Melanie, but I refused to believe he was doing anything with her. After all, it was his daughter and she was only twelve or thirteen.

"Melanie has a personality disorder. I don't know whether you knew that for not. She can't stand any kind of pressure. She really has no way to deal with it. I wanted to see what was going on myself one afternoon when we were alone. I stood next to her, very close. I could feel her agitation. She had to move away. By moving close again, I found that I could have her go anyway I wanted just by standing next to her. I herded her into my bedroom. When I took off my blouse, she also took of her blouse, continuing on undressing until she was totally unclothed, then she began fondling my breast. That's when I knew, where would she learn a response like that? I put my blouse back on and told her not to mention it to her father. He was my husband, I loved him, but I began to hate him a little too for what he had done to my daughter.

"In a way, I understood why he did what he did. Her youth and enthusiasm had to be a great temptation for him. After all, he wasn't really hurting her. He is the head of the house, a minister of God, the whole congregation respected him, I had to keep his secret or everything we had built would be lost. You know, it was my money that built that church. He used $80,000 of my money, everything I had inherited. And now it is all gone. I have no idea what to do next."

"Tell me about the boys."

"Pretty normal boys. They knew what was going on with their father and Melanie, but they never talked about it. It upset them though. Every once in a while, they would get into bed with me for comforting. They hadn't done that since they were three years old. It was all very innocent, they were just lonely and afraid. Boys being boys, sometimes they got a little handy, but I pushed them away and by the time they were ten, they were back in their own beds.

"Their father was taking more interest in them. Afternoons, they would go fishing, or drive to Yankton for the movies. As they spent more time with him, they seemed to grow up rapidly.

"I'm unsure about what to do now. I have a daughter who is lost without me in the room, and two boys who won't even talk to me most of the time."

"We are here to talk about you and the kids, not John."

"You're such an asshole, Frank. You are only acting sheriff, you know. You'll never get elected on your own."

"We've searched your house, Miriam. We know what's in your closet."

"Fuck you. You're another one out to judge me. What the hell would you know about comforting your children? So I let them have a feel sometimes, they were so afraid and lonely. Especially after

John would take them out for an afternoon. I never hurt them. They needed extra love."

"Did you feel Melanie needed extra love also?"

"All Melanie and I did was cuddle when she was feeling bad. All I ever did was try to protect my children. I'm leaving now."

After she left, Frank turned off the recorder. How could he have let this all happen without seeing it?

23
Matt

THE WEEDS HAVE been cut down in the driveway. Nice surprise for me as I drive up to the house. Sam Kelley must have hooked up his tractor and mowed them. The grass around the house has also been cut. The homestead looks good. Tomorrow, me and D'Angelo are going to have to break out the rakes to make this place look lived in.

I see D'Angelo staring intently at the computer through the kitchen window. He's set up at the table, lights on throughout the house, Coke cans litter the table, and a bag of chips has been opened and half dumped out. He looks up at me as I open the door, and the dogs start barking until they see it's me.

"Hey, Matt, got something here might interest you." He's pointing to a picture displayed on the computer screen. It's a photo of a car accident, two men are carrying a stretcher toward an ambulance, while a highway patrol officer watches.

The brightness of the screen makes it hard to see the grainy newspaper picture clearly.

"Who does this guy look like?" He asks, pointing to the man carrying the back of the gurney.

I study the picture intently. "Damn, D'Angelo, is that who I think it is?"

D'Angelo looks at me. "I think that's Dan Johnson right before he became Dan Johnson. The man in the stretcher, he's the real Dan Johnson, or at least he was. He just crashed his car and ended his life."

"How on earth did you ever find this?"

"Well, I was thinking we might as well check the fourth deputy since the search engine is paid for anyway." He takes the photo off the monitor and begins typing rapidly. "And I found this picture in the Peoria High School yearbook. This guy is the only Dan Johnson in their school." The computer monitor displayed the picture of a young man obviously not the Dan Johnson who was the deputy in Tindale.

He takes that picture down, his fingers bang away at the keyboard again, "And here is his picture at the University of Western Illinois in Macomb." It's the same picture as the graduate from Peoria High. "So then I got to thinking, how could Deputy Johnson assume the other guy's identity? I thought, maybe he died, so I checked the Illinois Record of Death, for Dan Johnson. He was killed in a car accident near Metropolis. I found the picture of the accident in the Metropolis News."

"Damn, D'Angelo, I think you cracked the case for us. Wonder how he ever got Dan Johnson's records?"

"I wondered about that too. I'm betting he lifted the guy's billfold, on the way to the hospital."

"Probably got into some serious trouble down there and took over Dan Johnson's identity. I believe we are looking at the real killer of Slug, Margo, John, and probably Javase. Now we got to figure out how to catch him. I'm calling Frank, to show him what you found. You are a genius D'Angelo, way to go."

"Frank, this is Matt out at the farm. Can you come out? D'Angelo has something to show you. We won't have to go out to Avon, I'll explain when you get here."

We showed our evidence to Frank, then checked Johnson's earnings record, which showed three years with no entries, then postings started again at an auto store in Des Plaines, Illinois. "We know who our killer is now. The man we knew as Dan Johnson is the bad guy. But how do we prove it?"

"It's going to be tough," said Frank. "We need to show that the body in the fire was not him, but there are no dental records for him, and any DNA evidence would have been destroyed in the fire. I know because DCI has already tried to prove his identity.

I think we have to discover the true identity of the man in the fire, or work at finding out the new name he's traveling under now. If I was doing it, I would get a homeless man from Sioux Falls or Sioux City and plant his body in the fire. Trouble there is that there's few records of the homeless that pass through, and very rarely do they have any dental records or DNA evidence available.

"So let's assume he did a repeat, and took the papers off a man who died in a car accident that Johnson attended while he was a deputy here. I will have Rosa pull those records, and we can go through them tomorrow."

Since it was already three, I told D'Angelo for our plans for the evening. He was less than excited.

"I know you're not much on meeting people, but this lady means a lot to me. Her response to you and the puppies is very important to me. Please come."

We stopped at the store and bought a thinly sliced pork tenderloin, a bottle of white wine, lemons, broccoli, and a few spuds. Loaded the car up with the groceries, puppies, and D'Angelo, and headed in for the evening. I was more than just a little worried.

We parked in the alley behind her house where the yard is fenced in, so we could let the hounds out. They raced through Sherry's backyard, delighted with any place new, and while they were bouncing rapidly from D'Angelo to me, she came out to greet us. She met Thunder first as he is fastest. He sniffed her once, lay at her feet, and rolled over for a tummy rub. Bogie was right behind him.

"The white lover there is Thunder. The little black guy is Bogie."

While she was busy petting them, D'Angelo and I walked up next to her.

"And this young man is a friend of mine, D'Angelo. D'Angelo, this beautiful lady is my friend, Sherry."

They were shaking hands and greeting each other, while I went back to the car for the bags of food.

Her kitchen is laid out perfectly. She put a mixer on the counter, while I started to heat a large frying pan on the stove. I laid the tenderloins in one layer on the bottom of the pan, and poured in a little white wine for them to sauté in. We chopped up the potatoes and started them cooking.

Sherry came over to stand next to me and watch. She hugged me, "I love your family, Matt. Thanks for bringing them over to me."

"I think of you as part of our family too. You know how much I care for you."

I turned back to the stove, flipped the tenderloins, covered them in wine again, and squeezed fresh lemon over the sizzling pork. I love the smell of cooking lemon. The potatoes were done, so we whipped them up, threw in a good dollop of butter, and put them on the table. Started the broccoli, pulled the tenderloins out, and displayed them on a platter. Poured another glass of wine in the pan to reduce, while I dished out the broccoli.

"Okay, we're ready, let's get the table set." I poured the wine sauce over the tenderloins and we all sat down.

Sherry took the first bite hesitantly, then a smile began, she looked up at me with a glowing face. "Wow, Matt, this is an awesome dish."

"Thanks, hope you both love it." D'Angelo looked up and smiled, but he's not one who will stop eating to talk.

Sherry and I loaded the dishwasher, while D'Angelo headed out to play with the dogs. We had poured another glass of wine and were sitting in the living room, when D'Angelo came in to say he was heading over to the bowling alley.

"Don't stay too late, Big Guy, we got a big day tomorrow." I heard the slam of a door and he was gone.

Sherry turned to me and smiled. "You know we need to talk, Matt."

"Oh dear, what did I do?"

"It's what you are going to do that worries me. You're going to leave and go back to Chicago. What about me while you're gone?"

"Chicago is where I live, Sherry. All vacations come to an end."

"I don't see why. What's so all fired great about Chicago? Let me tell you about last night, okay? After closing the bar, I took a long hot bath. In my backyard, I lit a white candle and watched the flames slowly consume it. I was concentrating my thought on you. Do you understand what I'm telling you, Matt? I'm telling you as plainly as I know how that I love you and want to be with you. Dammit, if you weren't such a stone headed turd who could pick up on a hint, I wouldn't have to be telling you this."

I took her hand in mine, "Sherry, I care deeply for you. I keep running into the same stone wall. You're a beautiful woman. Half the men in the county are in love with you, the other half just dream about you. I'm a washed up old man with nothing to offer. There are a ton of better prospects for you."

"You are such a fool. Do you really want to pick out a guy for me? Think I'm so stupid that I can't choose the right one for me?"

"I said that all wrong didn't I? I'm sorry. What I'm trying to say is that you're so young and vibrant while I feel more like a dried out old husk. What I don't want, more than everything in the world, is to hurt you."

Sherry was quite angry with me now. I could tell by the set of her jaw and the blaze in her eyes.

"I might not have graduated from high school and the world doesn't seem to be impressed by my intellect, but I know myself very well, and I know who I want. For Christ's sake, I am fifty years old and you're sixty-two. I'm not a fourteen year old virgin and you aren't on your deathbed. If we only have one year, or one week, or one day, I want it to be with you."

"I want to be with you also, but first you had to meet D'Angelo. You understand, don't you that, I plan on taking care of D'Angelo until he can make it on his own."

"I know that, I've talked to him already. I am going to study for my GED with him. I really want to get that diploma."

"And, I have to go back to Chicago to close down my apartment."

"Why didn't you tell me that before? I thought you was just going to go back."

"Actually, I am thinking of buying the farmhouse we're in now and fixing it up. I know D'Angelo loves it, kind of keeping it a surprise for him."

"Think there will be room out there for me?"

"My house will always have room for you, Sherry. But there is one more thing. I came out here to catch a killer. I haven't finished with that yet. I don't know how long it will take me."

"Help me here, why is he your responsibility?"

"Because he killed John Thatcher. Sheriff Thatcher saved my life once, I owe him this. I would go after him for that alone, but he's also a pedophile. He will begin abusing children as soon as he settles in a new area. Sexual abuse is a theft of their childhood. It casts their world into a dark evil place. Something I cannot abide.

One more thing, if I let him go, he could always come back for me and those I love."

"How long, you think?"

"Two weeks to a month. If I have to leave town, I'm hoping you'll kind of keep an eye on D'Angelo. He still needs a little help, but it would kill him to ask for it."

"You know I will, me and D'Angelo are going to be studying together."

24
Javase's Funeral

THE WHITE STONE church sits quietly in the afternoon sun. About a hundred people have gathered for Javase's funeral. We are still standing outside. The shock of another death, this time a well-liked young girl from the church, has delivered an unexpected blow to the health of the town. The immensity of the town's loss over the last month weighs heavily on everyone's thoughts. Today's services are being held by Pastor Ken from Yankton. He has been gracious enough to fill in until The Church of Christ the Savior can find another leader.

D'Angelo attends with me today. We have met more people now, and as we gather in the church yard, talking quietly to acquaintances, I see Sherry talking to the local banker and his family. D'Angelo and I slowly wander over that way.

"Hi, Matt. D'Angelo, let me introduce you to friends of mine. This is Penny Ann and George Selvitz, and their daughter, LeeAnn. We shake hands. D'Angelo and LeeAnn separate themselves slightly from the adults and begin talking about Javase. I notice that LeeAnn is talking sincerely about the loss of her best friend while standing very close to D'Angelo. She's a cute young blonde. He doesn't realize it yet, but he will have to be careful around that one. I believe she may have her cap set for him.

My attention distracted by D'Angelo and LeeAnn, I miss George's question to me until there is a long silence in our conversation. "I'm sorry, sir. My attention span is getting shorter every day. What did you ask me?"

"Sherry mentioned that you don't really believe Thurman is the person who killed Javase. I almost called him Pastor John again out of habit, but he was never a true pastor. He is an evil man."

"Sherry is right. I think the man who killed her has skipped town. He's probably hiding somewhere out west, under a different name. Still seems like everyone else, including the governor, thinks that Thurman is the murderer, and I have no proof of his innocence. There's a good chance they'll go for the death penalty."

Selvitz surprises me. "I think you're right. Everything was set up too neatly. Thurman never was all that smart if you ask me. He was a smarmy bastard who knew a lot of big words and could speak with firm conviction. Never did like him. Did I tell you about the time I caught him cheating at cribbage? Who cheats at a friendly card game?"

Penny Ann turned to face her husband, "I thought he was a nice man, just can't believe he killed anyone or was into child pornography. I hope they don't put me on the jury, because I refuse to believe he would kill anyone."

"He's guilty as hell of pornography, incest, and rape, for sure," said George. "I think they'll get him for a murder or two. Certainly seems he's guilty of killing Javase, anyway. She was so sweet, he should get a needle for her, if nothing else. And if you're right, another murderer is out in the west somewhere, probably hiding right in plain sight."

"Javase did seem like a sweet young girl. I can't understand anyone killing her. Just such a needless death. Tomorrow I'm heading out west to see if I can find him, but it seems like a really big haystack for a very well hidden needle," I say.

"Mr. Selvitz, I know this is a big change of subject, but could you do a favor for me? Would you talk to your friends over in Vermillion, and see if they will let D'Angelo take a few computer courses through USD while he is waiting to get his diploma?"

"Have him stop by the house later. LeeAnn already has the catalogue. She plans on taking a course after Christmas. Should be no problem at all."

After the funeral, the tears, and the gravesite, we went to Frank's office and watched while he pulled death records out of a folder and laid them across his desk.

"These are all of the automobile fatalities for the last four years. I started pulling a year before he began working here to make sure everything was included. Seven deaths total, but only two are men in the 25-40 year old range. Those two are Mark Emerson and Zachery Klynder. I checked the state database and couldn't find either of them living here in South Dakota."

Frank put their Social Security numbers up on the computer screen. No earnings posted on either record for the last two years. "Still," he cautioned us, "it can take a couple of years for earning to be posted to their records."

"Okay," I said, "let's consider the places or events where he could have access to another's identity. As an officer, he has many opportunities to access records like drunk drivers, accidents he attended, driver's license exams, and probably a hundred others I can't even think of. We have to find a way to exclude some of the people, or this will be a lifelong search."

Frank looked around at the office, shuffled the papers into one neat stack, and said, "Let's take a break and walk down to the bowling alley to get a Coke. I'm tired of being cooped up in this office."

The three of us sat around a table and looked at each other.

"If there is a way to come up with the name he is using, let me know. I personally can't think of any'" said Frank.

"Well," said D'Angelo, "How about the telephone calls? Is there any way to trace the 911 call about John Thurman or the message on Frank's answering machine about Javase?"

"The 911 came from a public phone, area code showed it to be out west. Nothing identifiable on the message left for me," said Frank.

"This is probably not the best time, but I'm going to take a short vacation, Frank. I think I'll head out to Yellowstone, take D'Angelo along to do a little fly fishing if he wants to go, and clear my brain out. When I come back, I'll be ready to catch him."

D'Angelo said, "Of course I want to go, I can help you drive."

"Sure, sure, you scurvy bastard, you go on vacation while I take all the heat," said Frank.

"There will be no heat for next couple of weeks, Frank."

"I know, just jerking your chain. Have a great time, see you in a couple of weeks."

Later that evening, D'Angelo and the dogs are back at the farm. Most of the town is dark. I knock on Selvitz's door. George opens it.

"Hey, Matt, come in please. I figured you'd be by."

We walk through the darkened house to the back porch, stopping to pick up a bottle of beer each. I light a cigar, offer him one which he declines, and we sit back on the lounge chairs.

"Want to tell me what's up, George?"

"I was hoping you would catch on, Matt. No one else ever seems to listen that much to what I say."

"Damn, George, if you were a dog, your tail would have been wagging. It was obvious to me that you wanted to tell me something. Do you know where he is, George?"

"I think he is in Cody, Wyoming, and he's going under the name Bill Benoit. That's the name and address he put on the envelope he sent to me." He handed me an envelope with a Postal Box number and a Cody, Wyoming, address. "I'm supposed to send him $5000 in the next two weeks, or he will release revealing photos of me with a minor. Do you think you can catch him?"

"I will get him, George. Can't promise that it will be in two weeks though."

"Would you like me to come along to help?"

"Nope, thanks anyway, but I prefer to work alone."

He handed me an envelope. "Here's $1000 to help you with your search. If everything comes out, so be it. It was my error, nobody else forced me. Should have relied on my love of Penny Ann, and not gotten carried away with lust. But that bastard should never have killed Javase. No way should she have been blamed."

"I'll take the money, George. No promises, hope I can get him in time."

The next morning D'Angelo was up early and had the coffee going. Puppies had eaten and were scrambling around in the front yard.

"How you like it out here now? Getting used to country sunshine?"

"What's not to like, Matt? I can ride my bike over to Lewis and Clark Lake in ten minutes and catch my first walleye five minutes later. There is a great campsite there I can park at and walk down to the lake. It's a beautiful place."

"Think you'd like to take some computer courses over at the University in Vermillion? I talked to Mr. Selvitz. LeeAnn will be taking a couple of courses after Christmas. Don't see why you couldn't too."

"I'd love that."

"Get the catalogue from LeeAnn tomorrow, and we'll set it up."

I did a lot of errands that next day. First I talked to Sam Kelley, then on his recommendation, to a carpenter-painter-handyman. I called Chicago and talked to my landlord. He is somewhat of a friend after renting from him the last several years. I bought burgers and potato salad for dinner with D'Angelo. We'd picked out a small hiba-chi, just the right size for us, and we both agreed that charcoal tastes better, especially when a few branches of Applewood are used.

D'Angelo had the university catalog from LeeAnn and was picking out classes that looked good to him.

"They have great courses, but everything I want requires me to take the simple classes first. I don't really need the easy classes. Is there any way I can get to the good stuff first?"

"My advice is to take two of the 101 classes. No matter how much you argue, they won't change their requirements. It will seem like a huge waste, but you'll get used to dealing with academia, and get a few credits that will help if you enroll full time later. You'll see, a university is like a nation unto its own self, it has its own language, and a ton of stupid, but rigid laws. The other thing is try to take classes that meet on the same day, and hopefully near the same time. That way when you drive over you can take two classes instead of having to drive every day.

"D'Angelo, I know you have a lot going on here, but I'm going to take a vacation and go out west. You can come if you want, or stay here and get ready for college. Totally your choice. If you bring your books, you can study on the way. I'm sure you'll be ready for the test in November either way."

"I'm coming along. We'll do some fishing, won't we?"

25
Cody

WE LEFT FOR Cody the next morning. The jeep was packed with camping gear. There was a new fly rod for D'Angelo, purchased at Leader's in Mitchell, which is just along the way on the interstate. We drove through the Badlands, then swung up to see Mount Rushmore near Rapid City. D'Angelo is a delight to travel with. Everything is new and enchanting to him. That said, he was pretty quiet looking over the side of the road as we went through the Bighorn Mountains. Finally, in the distance we could see Cody, Wyoming; the gateway to Yellowstone National Park.

We set up in an RV camp on the west side of Cody. They have a ton of room for tents and are dog friendly. They have a restaurant that serves up breakfast which is great for a couple of guys with only a hibachi. The next morning, we finished our eggs, two cups of coffee, and drove what I considered the most beautiful fifty miles in the world, the road between Cody and Yellowstone. The park is as wonderful as I recalled, and D'Angelo ate it up, from Old Faithful to being stuck for an hour in a herd of buffalo. The first day was so nice, we went back for day two: the paint pots, the geysers, and the waterfalls. Loved it all. The third day, the excitement continued with fast water and incredible trout.

The streams are fast, pristine, and loaded with great fish. D'Angelo and I are catch and release fishing only. The barbs on our hooks have been flattened, so the fish don't get injured by our fishing. We have enough to eat without consuming the fish of Wyoming. Incredibly, D'Angelo quickly picked up fly fishing. He can tie the knots, cast difficult casts, and land beautiful fish. He has not learned to match the hatch yet, but I'm sure he'll quickly learn. On the fourth day, I let him drop me in town while he headed out with the dogs to attack a small stream he saw. Time for me to begin looking for Johnson. I know that's not his name any longer, but it's easier to remember him by using his old name. I sit in a café across from the mailbox drop. I eat a second breakfast and have two leisurely cups of coffee. Probably have been watching the place for an hour and a half. That's enough watching for me. Johnson has not wandered in. Time to begin phishing.

The man behind the counter is resolute in his determination to tell me nothing. I tell him my friend has a box here and I want to leave him a message.

"Certainly, Sir. The easiest way to do that is to write him a note, put the number of the box on it, and I will place it in his box."

"Could you tell me which box belongs to Bill Benoit?"

"Sir, I do not know the names of the people that have boxes here. I keep track of the box numbers only."

I leave Mr. Sunshine and Light and walk to a local stationery store. I sit in the shade at the Buffalo Bill Center of the West and write a note to Bill, put it in an envelope, stamp it, and drop it in the local mailbox at the post office.

I walk back to the camp and light the charcoal in the hibachi. The western sky is starting to change the black shadows into soft purple hues as the heat begins to ease off. Right on time, D'Angelo rolls in and parks. While he feed the hounds, I throw on burgers and dogs. He reaches in the car, pulls out a ten pound bag of apples and a couple of bags of salad mix. He is obviously learning a little bit about nutrition.

That evening I tell him about the Buffalo Bill Center.

"Who was Buffalo Bill?" he asks.

"He was a famous cowboy and showman of the old west. Did you ever see any western movies or television shows?"

"No."

"How about the Seventh Calvary and the Battle at Little Bighorn?"

"Sorry Matt."

"Custer, Sitting Bull, how about Marshal Dillon?"

"Never heard of any of them."

"You'll know a lot more about them tomorrow, after we go through the museum."

Our fifth day was spent at The Buffalo Bill Center of the West where the Cody Firearm Museum is located. By the time we were done, D'Angelo learned a great deal about my childhood heroes, but I don't think any of them overly impressed him.

That evening when they were all in the tent and sleeping, I went to downtown Cody. I traveled from one bar to another, looking for Johnson. I saw nothing and finally just sat and drank a Bud while watching a late game on the tube.

She looks like a million dollars walking through the saloon door: early thirties, spring blonde hair, shapely hips, and long legs. She takes a seat at the bar next to me where I was sitting nursing a beer. I had been contemplating my next investigative move. And wham, she walks in and sits next to me. The heavens have opened and dropped its mana on me.

"Mind if I sit here?" she asked.

"I certainly don't, gorgeous. Want a beer?"

That's so sweet," she flashes me a smile that could have lit up most of Wyoming. "I'll have whatever you're having."

I raise my hand and hold up two fingers. The bartender brings us two more Buds.

I can't believe my luck. Here I am wondering what to do next and here she comes. At last a break. I have been noticed and I am worrying someone. I know this because, for the last fifty years, a woman looking like her has never hit on me. I really don't believe my looks have improved significantly in the last hour, so I'm safe to assume she is here for me. To make sure, I ignore her totally after the beer is delivered. I watch the televised game behind the bar, certain that she will initiate the action.

"Catch any fish today?" she asks.

"Nothing spectacular. Still it's great being down by the river. Say, how did you know I was a fisherman?" I have turned to face her with a look of surprise on my face.

"Not much else to do here. Yellowstone and fishing are the two biggies. Youdon't look like you are from around here."

"I did spend one day in the park. You're right, it's a great park. I get bored just looking at it, but I love the fishing here."

"I'm guessing there is other action you might really enjoy too, Matt," she says looking at me.

I take a long pull from my bottle. "What's your name, darling?"

She looks back at me. "You can call me Amber."

I've got my cell phone sitting on the bar. Fiddling with it nervously, I get it turned toward Amber and take her picture. I have the flash on, which of course surprises her.

"Why did you do that?"

"You're so beautiful, I wanted a picture."

"Delete it for me, please."

"Okay," I say, "I change the screen a little and push some buttons. "Oops. Damn, seems I transferred it to my computer and to Facebook. I always mess these electronic things up."

"That was stupid of you."

"Darling, that was not very seductive of you."

"I just want my picture off your phone, you stupid ass."

I reach into my pocket and take out my billfold. I count out five twenty dollar bills which I pat into a neat stack. "How did you know my name?"

"What are you talking about? If I know your name, it's because you said it."

I count out another hundred dollars in twenties, put this stack onto the first stack and push it toward her.

"Two hundred. Do you want it?"

"Are you suggesting I'm a prostitute?"

"Certainly not. I think you're a sweet young lady who has fallen madly in love with me and now wishes to slake the burning fire in her loins."

"You are nowhere near as funny as you believe you are."

I push the stack of twenties toward her. "This money is for you, but has nothing to do with action or even leaving the bar. I want the name of the man who sent you in here. Nothing else. And, I won't mention you were here."

"Nobody sent me here."

"I know and nobody told you my name. Well, Amber, the man who sent you in to try to get me out of the bar is trying to kill me. That's why I took your picture. If he succeeds, you will be an accessory to murder. So at some point here, you can drop the stupid act or just get up and leave."

She grabs my cell phone and pushes it deep into her purse.

"Sweetie, your picture is already on my computer, and on Facebook. You can have my cell phone if you really want it. Taking it won't provide you any protection. So here is my offer to you. Take the money and tell me his name. He is a bad guy who was not going to pay you anyway. You were going to be the victim I was supposed to have killed in the motel room before I killed myself. This man does not leave witnesses. And you know what he looks like, so he can't leave you alive. If you are smart, you'll take the money, tell me his name, and run somewhere safe. Hide until he is captured. Otherwise, the Cody police will be investigating your death before dawn breaks."

"You sure know how to kill an evening of fun, mister."

"There was never going to be any fun. It was an evening of work for you and a cold beer for me. You want another beer?"

"Yeah, as if I ever want a beer. What if I don't really know his name, I only know a name a friend called him?"

"What was he called?"

"Do I get the money?"

"Yes, but please give me back my phone."

She digs out my phone, flips it up on the bar, and picks up the money, "I heard a friend of his walking past call him Cy."

"Thanks Amber. Now take my advice and go somewhere safe, somewhere where he cannot find you."

"This really sucks. He said it was just a practical joke he was pulling on you and was going to give me a hundred dollars. Now I'm on your phone and some weird dude is after me."

I went back to our campsite, sat on a picnic table, and called Frank.

"I have my first lead. Johnson has seen me and he knows I'm after him. He sent in a girl to try to pick me up. It's proof that our shadow killer has been real all this time."

"You must have really spooked him. Wonder why he didn't just run again? Seems stupid for him to use violence, too close to a case already listed in the dockets. If he had just walked away, he would have been safe."

"Could be plain old retribution. We hurt him bad. We took away his golden nest, now he could just be trying to get even. I'm sending D'Angelo and the puppies home. I can't have him vulnerable while I'm hunting Johnson. I'll have my cell phone if you need to reach me. By the way, I have a name or at least a nickname for him. Seems his friends are calling him Tie."

D'Angelo argued, but I had him on the road by midnight. I told him to get a motel in an hour or so. My mind kept running scattered images of someone shooting into the tent with D'Angelo and the puppies in it. I'm unable to focus when I have to try to guard him.

Watching his tail lights disappear down Highway 16 to the east, I begin to walk west the two miles into Cody. I'm in a tourist town on the edge of Yellowstone National Park. Where would a killer best go to remain hidden? I stop at the first motel on the outskirts of the city and get a room on the second floor. I want the second floor as I doubt Tie will check beyond the first floor. Still, if I am mistaken and get trapped, a jump from the second floor will probably not kill me.

I begin to work it out while I drink a soft drink from the machine outside the office. Tie has to have a place to conduct business and yet remain unknown. I strip down, put the shower on hot, and begin shampooing my hair. Twenty minutes later I crawl into bed with the answers starting to come slowly.

The best way for him to remain hidden is to not live in the same town as his mail drop. It's impossible to trace him through the mailbox, so the easiest and probably the fastest way to find him is to check out the towns close to Cody. I have already checked the town of Cody and all the nearby towns for the name Tie, and have found nothing. I could set up surveillance on the business where is drop box is located, but he may come in only every several months. I can't bear waiting that long just watching something.

26
The Killer

THE KILLER VISITED his mail drop during his noon hour and found the note left by Matt Smith. "I'm coming for you Johnson," was all it said. There seemed no way that he could have been tracked here. The front of the envelope listed his name as Bill Benoit. The only one who had that name and his mailbox number was Selvitz, and he certainly wouldn't have said anything. Still here he was. Fuck Selvitz, I'm mailing off the pictures incriminating him tomorrow. If George told Smith, he wouldn't be paying hush money anyway.

Best thing to do is to leave now. Smith didn't know his name or where he was. Cut the ties to the past and start new. But that was the thing, if he could get rid of Smith, he could try to milk Selvitz again. George wouldn't be so brave if Smith died out here.

He was just getting off work when he saw Smith leave the museum where the killer worked. Now that he had a bachelor's degree in history, he had quickly been put on the staff. Authority figures always believed what they see printed on paper. His interview was a farce, they wanted to talk about how wonderful life was out here, trying to convince him to work here, rather than see if he was qualified.

He spent the evening in the shadows, watching for Matt. When he did locate him, the killer followed him until he finally sat and ordered a beer. He called his co-worker Brenda. This was the kind of work she could do best and she had been complaining that she needed extra money.

Brenda was more than happy with the hundred dollar bill and was willing to help him with the practical joke. Somehow, things didn't work right. She was unable to get him to leave the bar, and when she did come out, she told him that Matt had taken her picture and told her that he was a bad man.

"Oh, Brenda, you should have listened to him," he said as he twisted her head slightly, then snapped her neck and let her drop. Maybe the police would find her body, associate her with Matt, and find her picture on his cell phone. Who knows, the damned police ought to be good for something, sometime.

27
Matt

I WALK DOWN to the drop box in the morning. Mr. Sunshine is behind the counter.

"Anyone leave a message for me?"

"I take messages in written form for my customers only."

"That's swell. I will consider it a 'no'. You have a good day now," I say as I turn to leave.

I cross the street to the café, have another wonderful breakfast and several cups of coffee.

If Tie has a job, he probably stops in on his noon hour to check for mail. Given that he received a message from me yesterday, I'm certain he won't be returning until he knows that I've left town. He may have checked the campgrounds around Cody and discovered that I have checked out of the RV site. Maybe he thinks he chased me out of town.

The car rental office at the Yellowstone Airport arranges to pick me up, and I've got wheels again. It's time to begin my search of the outlying towns where he is probably living. Looking at a map, I cross off the towns west of Cody. They are too busy with traffic to the park. A small town to the south, Dry Creek, seems like a good place to start, but doesn't sound like much of a fishing hole. Sitting in a shady spot in the town park, watching the traffic come and go, I finished off a six pack of bottled water. That evening I dine on tacos and spend the night in a local motel. Tomorrow will hopefully be productive.

After burritos and coffee for breakfast, I head north through Cody, all the way to Kamm's Corner. Find another shady spot, refill my cooler, and begin my vigil. I take a break at two o'clock and walk to the bar behind me for a frosty. I need beverages that don't taste like water. I light a cigar, take a long pull off the beer, and the bartender comes right over.

"Let me guess, no smoking?"

"I don't give a fuck if you smoke. This is the west, our laws aren't made by health freaks in California. In fact, I was hoping to bum one off you, haven't had time to run over to the station yet."

"Be delighted to give you one." I dug out my little pack, and my new buddy, Sam, lit up and began to tell me all about Kamm's Corner.

"Mostly we are a place to go through to get to Cody or Powell, but Al's gas over there has good prices, so a lot of them fill up here, and I serve drinks and cold beer. Got a pretty steady clientele during the week. On the weekends, we get a few fishermen. The road out east of town leads to a small lake fed by the river. Good fishing. There is even a trailer park there with a half dozen trailers set up by people who come on the weekends. Not really such a bad place if you like quiet, and I like quiet. After working in Las Vegas for twenty years, I bought this place. After about a year my wife left me, and it was really quiet then, if you know what I mean."

"Sounds like a perfect life for me," I said. "I'll probably take a look at the lake before I leave town. Man, I love to fish."

"The bait shop is closed. It's only a weekend thing."

"No problem," I say, "just going to look."

I packed my gear into the Camry, drove behind the bar and followed a rustic path a half mile or so down to the lake. Five mobile homes parked in a sad little line to the left side of the road. I turned around, so I wouldn't get the Camry stuck. After wandering down by the tiny swamp the bartender had called a lake, beating at the mosquitos, and heading back to my car, I wondered again at the twisted perception of reality that local residents can have. I noticed a car with a small boat trailered behind it coming down the path and stepped off into the weeds so it could pass. It stopped right next to me, window rolled down, and I was looking down the barrel of a pistol held by Dan Johnson.

"Step back, lay down on your face, and put your hands behind you."

He taped my hands together, ripped off a piece of duct tape, covered my mouth, then pulled me up and walked me to the last mobile home.

"Nice to see you again, Matt, you miserable bastard. I should kill you right now, but I want to take my time. Get on that bed."

I lay on the bed before me. He taped my hands, this time to a maple headboard, taped my legs to the bed frame, then covered me over with blankets.

"That should keep you for a couple of hours. But here, just so you have a taste of what's coming." He hit side of my head with his pistol and everything went black.

I fight hard to get back to the light. It's just ahead of me. I reach for it. Light is life, dark is eternal quiet. It's difficult to breathe. I pull at my hands, they move just a little. My legs are cramping, I am unable to move them. The strip of duct tape covering my mouth is too long. One end is loose and has bent itself up to the side of my nose, impairing my ability to breath. I rub my face against my shoulder attempting to dislodge the tape. Little help that. I jerk my legs up with as much force as I can muster. They move about two inches. I do the same with my arms, and there is a little more slack there. This time I move three inches. I arch my back, lift my body as far off the bed as possible, then fall back. Nothing gives in the bed. Still, I remember my three year old daughter jumping on my bed long enough to break it, and she was less than thirty pounds. I spend five minutes doing my best to bounce on the bed. Maybe it's a little more flexible. Resting from that, I begin jerking my right hand down as hard as I can, trying to stretch the tape. My left arm is still too sore after being shot the month before to pull very hard. I listen intently in the dark, and hear nothing. I think the bed will be the weak link here, and begin lifting myself up and dropping back onto the bed.

Stop to listen, hear nothing, lift, drop. How much longer do I have? How long have I been unconscious? I can't weaken now. I jerk hard with my right arm, five hard pulls, lean my right leg into the tape, contract the muscles as tight as I can, lean into my left leg, and do the same. I relax, then snap both legs hard; maybe there is a little give. I arch my back, throwing myself off the mattress a few inches, then flop back as hard as I can. It's possible that the bed frame is starting to weaken, but it is difficult to judge how much more it's sagging.

I hear a knock at the front door. I remain quiet trying to hear. Then grunt as loudly as I can. Hell, there is no way anyone can hear me, but I try to thrash around on the bed and squeal. Bounce, bounce, bounce, whoever you are, listen to this bed bouncing around in here. You probably think he's having sex. Open that door whoever you are.

The knocking stops. Everything is silent. I hear a car start. Don't go, come back, pull me out of here. I hear a sound like someone pulled the front door off, and then a man shouting, "Come out here Johnson, you bastard. Time for you to die."

I see a light go on down the hall. I bounce the bed and grunt, and then hear approaching footsteps. The overhead lights go on and I'm blinded. I blink hard, while my eyes adjust. He pulls the tape from my mouth. Gratefully I take a deep breath.

"George? Is that really you, George?"

"In the flesh. Came out to help get Johnson." He cut through the tape binding me to the bed frame and helped me stand up. It took a few minutes to work the blood back into my arms and legs. At last I could move without pain.

"Do you have any weapons with you, George?"

"Yes, I have my pistol and a couple of skinning knives. My pistol is a Jennings .22."

"Get it loaded and cocked, in case he comes through that door. Let me have one of the knives. How did you ever find me?"

"The GPS on your phone. D'Angelo and LeeAnn have been talking, she has your cell phone number, so I called Rosa and she was able to locate you. I'm not sure you want me here, but this is my responsibility too."

"You saved my life, George. Trust me, I want you here, welcome aboard. He's going to come back here soon, and we are going to kill him tonight."

"Won't we get in trouble with the law?"

"He is already dead. Can't get in trouble killing a man who has already burned to death. Besides, George, you and me are world class liars and neither one of us has ever been here. Your choice though, you want to stay and wait with me, or head into Cody and I'll join you later?"

"I'm with you for the whole thing. No big adventure in Cody."

We pulled the door back into place on the frame, turned off the lights, and sat there in the dark, waiting for Johnson to come back. It was 9:00 p.m.

George kept talking to me, but he spoke softly so I didn't stop him. He'd seen D'Angelo back in Tindale and knew I'd found Johnson, that's why he drove out. He'd told Penny Ann about Javase, so he might be getting divorced. Penny Ann had been silent as he prepared to come out to Cody. LeeAnn and D'Angelo seemed to be keeping company, and it was okay with him. D'Angelo seemed like a nice young man.

At 12:30 a.m. I gave it up for the night. I couldn't take any more talking or waiting. "Something spooked him, George. He won't be back again tonight."

"Back to Cody?"

"I want you to wait here. I'm going out the back door to make sure he's not sitting out there waiting for us. When I start the Camry and honk the horn, come out. If someone walks in that door, shoot him, because it won't be me. You understand?"

"Yes, Camry and horn."

I searched around in the dark until I was sure, then honked for George. We picked up his Cadillac, drove to the airport, returned my Camry, and went to the Holiday Inn for the night.

"You know, George, I used to be quicker, but it has finally come to me. Could be the guy was calling him Ty, like in Ty Cobb. Al and Janet's last name was Cobb. Johnson took the identity of their son, Jacob Cobb. We could get ahold of Frank tomorrow and ask him to put out a bulletin here in Wyoming to help locate him. We would find him faster that way, but remember, Frank is the law. If they capture him, he'll go back and stand trial and probably will end up riding a needle into eternity. Or he might get off."

"Let's get him ourselves, Matt. What do you say?"

"I agree, get some sleep now, we are out of here in three hours."

I shook him awake at 4:00 a.m. We were on our way back to Kamm's Corner. By 4:45 we were in place behind a copse of trees on the east side of the road. Now, he just had to come by. I prayed he had not disappeared again. My hope was that he had not had time to establish another identity and would be hesitant to leave without a new place to settle in.

At 6:15 he drove past. We started on his trail.

"You a good shot with your pistol, George?"

"Nobody is a good shot with a Jennings."

"What I'm saying here is, do you want to drive or shoot?"

"I'll drive."

I checked the load, the Jennings carries seven rounds in its clip. I racked a shell into the chamber, "Time for you to pass him and take him fast, just over this hill. Now, George, put that hammer down. Give it all you can."

I cock the Jennings, roll down my window, and as George swings out into the left lane closing in fast on the BMW, I aim at Johnson. He spots us as we near him, and his rear tires begin to smoke as he steps on the gas. I shoot at the window. No chance I hit him, the angle was too difficult. I lower my aim and shoot at the front tire. After three quick rounds the Jennings jams, and we revert to the roll of spectators.

"Back off, George. Slow down, the gun's jammed."

The BMW swerves into the left lane, sails down into the ditch, and crashes through the fence. It continues across the field to a stand of trees which wander down the far fence line toward the small lake.

"Pull over and stop, George."

"I can run him down. We can't let him escape."

"George," I said, "this Cadillac is not going to pass between those trees, so we will have to run him down on foot. He's younger, faster, knows where he's going, and he may be armed. Just pull over and turn around. We need to beat him to his mobile home." George hurried it down the narrow road. No sign of Johnson near the small lot of mobile homes.

In the pink light of early dawn, we entered the trailer, and turned all the lights on.

"What are we looking for?" asked George.

"Anything that will help us find him." I searched through the kitchen cabinets, pulled open every drawer in the kitchen and bedroom, flipped the mattress off the bed, searched through the bathroom, and found nothing. Finally, I lifted several of the ceiling tiles and looked in the narrow space under the metal roof. In a small package above the bathroom, I found two banded bundles of money, and a bag of jewelry.

"Here," I threw a package to George, "your share of the swag. We'll return the jewelry to Frank. It was probably stolen from Janet, but the cash can't be tracked."

"Is that honest?"

"You're the church member, you tell me. One of the things I learned early in life is that if you find cash, put it in your pocket. If you don't want it, toss it over to me. It's probably the money they took off you anyway."

He stuck it in his pocket.

"Let's get out of here," I said.

We drove back to the BMW in the field. No Johnson anywhere around. I jumped out, got the tire wrench out of George's trunk, walked over to the BMW, broke the windshield, punched a hole in each tire, busted a hole in the gas tank, and went back to the Cadillac.

"He won't be driving that anywhere today. Let's head back into Cody for breakfast." On the way into town, I reloaded the Jennings.

We sat in the café across from the mail drop. I ordered a large country fried steak breakfast and coffee, but George was too nervous to eat.

"Matt, I have to know what we are doing next."

"George, we're doing it now."

"I don't mean eating, I mean how are we going to locate Cobb?"

"I'm not really eating, I'm using the food as a disguise while I'm undercover. You're busy watching that mail drop. That's one place he won't leave town without checking. So you watch until he shows, or we begin searching here in Cody again. While you do that, I'm going to watch that Wells Fargo over there. I don't know for sure that it is his bank, but it stands to reason that he would bank near where his mail drop is located. He was always careful and plotting, he wouldn't want to walk too far carrying a lot of cash."

"You know, Matt, I'm starting to have more trust in you all the time. Now, where is that waitress, might just as well at."

The tiny café is laid out with four booths against the street side of the building. There is a counter with ten stools, with an opening in the middle of the counter for the waitress. The coffee and beverage station is located on the left behind the counter, the desserts and pastries on the right. There is no door to the kitchen and a shoulder high opening across the back gives the cook a place to set the completed orders. After the waitress takes George's order, I go to the restroom to wash my hands. They feel grimy after digging through the mobile home.

As I come out of the restroom, I see Johnson with a gun in his right hand, walking from the kitchen toward George. No time to think, I draw and fire the Jennings before he can get a round fired off at George. I am less than ten feet from him, but the Jennings is not known for accuracy. The .22 doesn't carry much punch, but luckily I hit his forearm and his gun slumped a bit.

George glances both ways quickly, there is no escape. He rises from the booth and goes for Johnson with his butter knife. I am going at him as fast as I can, but George is closer and jumps him first. Johnson hits him hard in the face, but George's motion keeps him going forward. George wraps his arms around the man's legs, taking all of Johnson's attention. I pick up and throw the half-full coffee pot at him. The hot liquid splashes onto his face and he screams. I follow the coffee pot with the steak knife, but I tripped, falling on my right shoulder, rolling to the left, I stab upward desperately with the knife and I am in luck. I bury the knife deep into his crotch. Johnson stopped immediately. Both hands moving rapidly to his wound. I jam the bag of Janet's jewelry into Johnson's pocket, grab George and pull him away from the man's legs, and the two of us escape out the front door before the authorities arrive. We take the first corner to the left, then drive out of town, heading east and checking in the rearview mirror as we drive.

"How do we know if we got him?" George asks.

"We got him in the hospital. Anyway, Frank will be able to find him there. Let's just get the hell out of here before we end up in jail."

"Matt, did you see me? I attacked him. Did you see? Damn, I sure wish Penny Anne had been there to see me."

"You were some kind of fierce beast, George."

28
Christmas

SHERRY HAS LARGE joint of beef in the oven. It's been slowly roasting since early morning and the house smells great. There is a large bowl of whipped potatoes with large pats of butter melting down its sides and a pan of dressing made heavy with beef juices. While D'Angelo and Sherry handle the food, appetizers, and a salad, I have been hard at work finding a punch bowl, a dozen eggs, and vanilla ice cream. We now have fresh eggnog for the afternoon. I've sampled three cups, and believe it is the best I've made.

We have a Christmas tree set up in the living room with Sherry's lights and decorations, supplemented with homemade ornaments from D'Angelo and me. Weeven put up lights one afternoon on one of the apple trees in our orchard. I love the Christmas spirit D'Angelo is infusing into everything.

I can see a car pull into our driveway. It's Frank's old Chevy. Close behind him is the Selvitz's Cadillac. We greet them at their cars. D'Angelo helps George and Penny Ann unload their car and carry all the goodies into the house.

"It's wonderful having you all here," I shout. "Come in, come in, get to know us better. This house is the ghost of Christmas present."

D'Angelo and LeeAnn are already outside, walking close together and discussing the important things that the young always discuss, or maybe they are trying to get away from the Perry Como that I have on the stereo.

Frank filled us in on the upcoming trial of the man we knew as Dan Johnson.

The DNA under Javase's fingernails was a match, and the jewelry had been proven to be Janet's. Frank seemed confident Johnson would be sentenced to life without the possibility of parole.

Later George came over to talk to me. He was worried that at some point Johnson would be released from jail.

"I know what you're saying, George, but I think I have solved that possibility. See that stack of gifts over there?" I pointed at twenty wrapped packages. "Those are going to be mailed out on Monday to inmates at the prison Johnson is going to. Each contains a carton of cigarettes, a picture of Johnson, and a short note describing the injury to his genitals. Hell, he will be the closest thing to a woman many of them will ever see again. He won't last a month."

It was an afternoon of excess. Too much food, too much drink, way too many presents, but just the right amount of good friends. At the start of our meal, I raised my glass. "I want make a toast to you all. You have shown us that family and friends are everything. May our lives, however long they may be, have many more days of such happiness as I feel today."

By early dark, with the room lit by the merriness of the tree lights, I nodded off. D'Angelo shook my shoulder to wake me.

"You probably don't think all this is very important, Matt, but this house and the Christmas tree, are more than I ever even dreamed of. You really gave me a chance at life with your belief in me."

"How nice of you to say. But D'Angelo, you have blessed my life by becoming my friend." I stand up and give him a hug. "George gave me the good news already that your loan has gone through, so next week you'll be starting college."

"Matt, can you really see me as a collegiate?"

"I absolutely can. I think when you put forth the effort, you can do anything. You won't be too far from home in Vermillion, and you know I will take good care of Thunder while you're away. I think you only have to be on campus for the first two years. I'm hoping you'll come back on some of the week-ends."

D'Angelo looked away, then rose and picked up the coffee pot. He filled both of our cups. "I really don't want to be separated from you and Bogie and Thunder that long, but trust me, I'll be back a lot."

"Well, Merry Christmas and Happy New Year, D'Angelo. I'm sure glad we met this summer."

"Me too, Matt. I told LeeAnn I would take her bowling. See you later, unless you and Sherry want to come around."

"Maybe later, have a good time."

Sherry came into the room and sat behind me. "It's been my best Christmas ever, Matt. Glad you two came to town. I really love that D'Angelo, he's a great guy."

"I love him too, but us guys can't say that kind of shit."

"George told me that the loans have been approved for him at college. You know, I will pay his tuition for him if he needs it."

"Thanks Sherry, but I know he will do it himself. Here, let me show you what he will get as a graduation present." I went upstairs to our bedroom and opened my top drawer. I handed her a watch. "How do you like it?"

"All you plan on giving him for graduating college is a watch?" she said incredulously.

"Did you look at it?"

"It looks nice."

"Sherry, that's a Hublot watch. He will be able to sell that watch for upwards of fifty thousand dollars."

"No way, what makes it so valuable?" You know I'm a gambler, Sherry, and you know I usually win. I happen to be a very good gambler. I won that watch together with this gold bracelet when I won the World Poker Tour out in Vegas. So don't worry about D'Angelo too much. Between us, we'll give him a good start. Now, darling, D'Angelo starts school in two weeks. How would you like a short vacation to Florida or Costa Rica for some fishing and sun?"

"I can't, Matt. I've signed up to start college too, but I'd sure like to spend the afternoon bowling with you. Let's take that trip together as my graduation gift."

Made in the USA
Charleston, SC
11 April 2016